106

ON THE HEAD OF A PIN

Mary
Beth
Miller

Dutton
Books

Dutton Books

A division of Penguin Young Readers Group

Published by the Penguin Group

Penguin Group (USA) Inc., 375 Hudson Street, New York, New York 10014, U.S.A. / Penguin Group (Canada), 90 Eglinton Avenue East, Suite 700, Toronto, Ontario, Canada M4P 2Y3 (a division of Pearson Penguin Canada Inc.) / Penguin Books Ltd, 80 Strand, London WC2R 0RL, England / Penguin Ireland, 25 St Stephen's Green, Dublin 2, Ireland (a division of Penguin Books Ltd) / Penguin Group (Australia), 250 Camberwell Road, Camberwell, Victoria 3124, Australia (a division of Pearson Australia Group Pty Ltd) / Penguin Books India Pvt Ltd, 11 Community Centre, Panchsheel Park, New Delhi - 110 017, India / Penguin Group (NZ), Cnr Airborne and Rosedale Roads, Albany, Auckland 1310, New Zealand (a division of Pearson New Zealand Ltd) / Penguin Books (South Africa) (Pty) Ltd, 24 Sturdee Avenue, Rosebank, Johannesburg 2196, South Africa / Penguin Books Ltd, Registered Offices: 80 Strand, London WC2R 0RL, England

This book is a work of fiction. Names, characters, places, and incidents are either the product of the author's imagination or are used fictitiously, and any resemblance to actual persons, living or dead, business establishments, events, or locales is entirely coincidental.

The publisher does not have any control over and does not assume any responsibility for author or third-party websites or their content.

CIP Data is available.

Published in the United States by Dutton Books,
a member of Penguin Group (USA) Inc.
345 Hudson Street, New York, New York 10014
www.penguin.com/youngreaders

Designed by Heather Wood
Printed in USA   First Edition
ISBN 0-525-47736-5
1   3   5   7   9   10   8   4   2

For Ben, who told me about the deer,
and for Tess, Luke, Nathan, and Jake

ALSO BY

MARY BETH MILLER

Aimee

ACKNOWLEDGMENTS

I want to thank all the hairdressers in the world for telling their one-line stories, "Did you hear . . . ?" so that writers like me could turn them into novels. I also am grateful for the support of my friends who helped me through a difficult editing process: Sue Beckhorn, Olga Snyder, Lana Snowman, Sian Packard, Brenda Bonczar, Ronnie Schenkein, the Reverend Elaine Silverstrim, the RACWI members, and the YAWriters.

I want to thank Stephanie Owens Lurie for the times she was right and for putting up with me when I thought I was right. Thanks also to Andrea Brown for her staunch support. Without it there would be no *Pin*. To Luke, Nathan, Ben, Tess, and Jake, thank you for your patience when I was deep into the book and off in my own world.

Author's Note

The prayer that begins Joshua's chapters is called the *Confiteor* (or "I Confess" in English). It's been part of the Roman Catholic Mass since the tenth century, achieving its current form by the sixteenth century. The *Confiteor* asks forgiveness for the supplicant's sins from God, his angels and saints, and from other people. It can be found in any Roman Catholic Sunday Missal or on the Internet.

Michael's chapters begin with verses from a 2,500-year-old school of thought called Taoism. The basic tenet of the *Tao Te Ching* is nonaction. It emphasizes the natural over the unnatural and the seeking of peace or inaction in the face of violence or action. There are thousands of translations of the *Tao Te Ching*. Each translation is different because of the evolution in the meaning of the original Chinese symbols from ancient times to the present and because the verses were written with latitude built in for personal interpretation. Even the order of the poems has been disputed. I've used the newer numerical system, quoting from: Lao Tzu, *Tao Te Ching: Mystical Classics of the World*, translated and annotated by Victor H. Mair; New York: Quality Paperback Book Club and Bantam Books, 1998; Verse 67 (22 in the old numbering), p. 87, and verse 77 (33), p. 100.

Psalm 23 is from the King James Bible.

ON THE HEAD OF A PIN

Opening Prayer/Processional

The Lord is my shepherd;
I shall not want.
He makes me to lie down in green pastures:
he leads me beside the still waters.
He restores my soul:
he leads me in the paths of righteousness
for His name's sake. . . .
Psalm 23: 1–3

Andy shouts as I walk into the party, "Hey! It's Helen! Let's all bow and grovel!" He's referring to my being this year's homecoming queen. His eyes dance wicked circles across his audience's faces.

Vying for the status of the girl most guys want to screw and girls want to imitate wasn't something I enjoyed. It wasn't until Michael told me to go for it that I'd agreed, but the dance was miserable. The girls chattered about who was too fat for her dress and who was panting after someone else's date. Michael had looked like he wanted to run but had nowhere to go.

I don't primp, preen, or sulk about my newly won honor like Andy wants, so he goes back to what he does best: entertaining. Actually, he's the one acting like small-town royalty. His mouth flaps like a duck's ass—my dad's favorite phrase—while he guzzles a cheap beer. Andy goes on and on about the king, his father.

"It all started," Andy says, "at my party last winter. The one where that freshman drank too much and had to have his stomach pumped."

Several boys nod. Several more swig beer. Only Josh Stedman remains still, except for his lips. Part of me thinks Josh's praying for Andy to shut up. The room reeks of spilled beer, alcohol breath, soggy chips, and sweat, with a hint of vomit. I never like coming to a party late unless I've had a few.

"This guy at the party said his car's air conditioner was broken." Andy's in the boasting stage of his drunk, not far from the staggering point. He may not even make it to the end of his story if he emphasizes the main points with too many gulps of beer.

My shoulders tense, and Michael massages them as though he can hear what I'm thinking. He knows me better than a dog knows his own privates, which is another of Dad's phrases. Michael says into my ear, "Not this story again. I'm finding something to drink. What do you want, Helen?"

"Whatever," I say. "Just not beer."

I can't take my eyes off Andy. He's not drop-dead gorgeous, but he's close. He smiles at a girl, and she melts. But not me— Andy isn't my type. Besides, he acts exactly like how I imagine Dad did at my age, trying too hard to impress people.

What would I be like if I'd been born the boy Dad wanted? Would I be an Andy or a Josh or a Michael? Maybe I'd be one of the wannabes flocking around Andy, telling jokes bordering on porn to watch a prude's reaction, or smacking heads to see who's tougher. Like it matters. I'll always be a girl, and Dad will continue to be disappointed in me until death do us part.

"We decided," Andy continues, after shouting down a belching contest, "to take some Freon from the fridge, figuring he didn't need much to get his air conditioner working again. We were drunk, or I'd have told the guy to just open his car window. It *was* winter." He waits for a laugh. The guys give it to him, all except Josh. He's staring over Andy's head, past me.

I swing around slow and see Victor Munger, the class time bomb, on the porch. Someday, somebody will say the wrong thing, and Victor will blow. I don't intend to be around when he does. I edge farther into the room, staying within story range.

"When we hauled the fridge away from the wall, we nearly gagged. You wouldn't believe the shit that accumulates behind a fridge, especially out here in the woods. Dead mice husks were everywhere. They looked like they'd been mummified. And the mouse crap! The mice had dumped so often, the floor was crunchy. We had to push the fridge against the counter before this guy could look for the Freon. I let him take care of that, but I shouldn't have. A couple of *shits* and *damns* came from behind the fridge, but even then I didn't check on him. He left carrying something, but I didn't know whether he'd actually drained any Freon or not. It wasn't until later that I remembered his hair looked icy. Anyway, I had to shove the fridge back myself because he skipped out."

Andy glances at Josh's empty hands, but Josh doesn't notice. Josh hasn't been smashed since his sister's accident. Come to think of it, he hasn't had any fun since then. He's been all prayers and church services, somber eyes and devoted son. Almost like a kid who's making up for something.

Andy's mouth is off and running again. "Well, I didn't come back to the cabin for a month. Then I came with Dad." Grins and groans greet the mention of Mr. Grabbit. "He was planning a snowmobile party with a bunch of out-of-town dickheads. You know, the guys who come up here and pretend they know the woods?"

Michael slips a bottle into my hand and tries to lead me away, but I'm trapped by the inevitability of Andy's story. This one, like his others, will end with some gross, supposedly wonderful act on his father's part. Yet, here we stand, listening like a paying audience.

"Dad wanted the place cleaned up, because he needed to impress these guys. He took the kitchen and gave me the bathrooms, jerk. Like I know how to clean a toilet, or I'm actually going to do it." He pauses for his laugh track. When it arrives on cue, he says, "I never had to, either, because Dad was bellowing like a cow with a calf turned backward."

Michael whispers, "Like he's been on the same side of a fence as a cow."

I elbow him and stifle my laugh. Michael never wanted to be part of the in group, not even before he graduated. He's always cracking irreverent lines.

"Turns out the guy had cut the Freon thingie wide open. What he didn't take ran onto the floor, where it made mouse-shit soup and ruined the linoleum, not to mention the fridge. Everything was spoiled. It stunk like a rotting skunk."

He chugs half his beer while the guys chuckle at his latest "funny."

"Dad made me push the fridge onto the porch. I left it about where Munger's standing now. Then he ordered new flooring and appliances. He wanted the stove and fridge to match, so he bought both." This is to remind us that Andy doesn't have to worry about money like the rest of us.

"When we came back a few days later, the fridge door was off its hinges and lying in the yard. The food had been eaten, and the containers—plastic, glass, aluminum—shredded. A bear had visited, which shouldn't have surprised us since Dad has his own personal dump out back."

Which is illegal, but Andy doesn't care if his dad gets in trouble for dumping trash.

"Dad set a big jar of peanut butter on the old fridge to lure the bear back. The bear didn't wait for dark like Dad expected. It showed up for dinner. It ate the peanut butter, but it could smell better things cooking inside the cabin. It took less than a minute for it to tear the back door off its hinges and lumber in."

Several girls gasp, and Andy bloats with storyteller's pride.

Victor moves into the light. His grin is laced with scorn. He creeps me out worse than any bear.

"What'd you do?" squeals a girl.

"I ran for it. I want to make it to twenty whole, you know? I figured that the bear wouldn't come upstairs, so I made for the farthest bedroom."

He acts like this isn't cowardly, but Victor, slithering ever closer, says, "What? Mr. Tough Guy didn't take on the bear with a kitchen knife?"

I can almost see Victor's hand groping for his knife. He wears these steel-toed boots his dad gets at work for free, and he uses them in fights. Broke a kid's ribs last year, then told the whole school he did it. He also let it be known that he keeps a "blade" tucked in his boot.

"Shut up, moron. I'm not stupid," Andy says. Only he would insult Victor like that. I don't know where he finds the guts.

Andy's been hanging with Victor more and more. None of us can figure out why. Poor Josh is left in that awkward position of sticking with them or finding a new friend in a high school class of only seventy kids. With Josh going holy and Andy running wild, it'd be logical if they parted. But they've been friends since they were babies.

"Helen," Michael says, "let's find someplace quiet."

"In a minute," I say, remembering the stories Moshie tells the kids who hang at his store. They're always about people who've done stupid things. "Think," he says. "Think before you do something. Is what you're about to do worth the embarrassment of being caught or having the police after you?" Andy's story will be a good one to tell Moshie. He's obviously building up to something massively stupid.

"The bear didn't make it to the kitchen. My dad grabbed a gun and blew it out the back door." He points at a skinny door. "I didn't even know he kept a gun in there."

"In here?" Someone opens the door, which leads to a pantry.

"Yeah," Andy says. He straightens as though his dad took out four terrorists instead of a hungry bear. "He walked *toward* the bear to grab the gun."

Michael pulls me away, and I let him. I don't want to hear how many shots it took to kill it. I take a long drink of my wine cooler to banish the image of a bear lying dead on the floor.

"You shouldn't have listened," Michael says after he's secured a place on the sofa close to the fire. "It's only bravado anyway. No bear came in the house. The guys at the shop said Mr. Grabbit shot it on the porch, then unscrewed the hinges to make it look like it had come inside."

"He still shot it, Michael. What's the difference?"

"The truth. If Mr. Grabbit hadn't done something to make it look like the bear was coming after him, he'd have been in trouble for hunting out of season."

I nod, swallow more of my drink, then try for a subject change. "Have you been painting lately?" Michael's the best painter I know, and I'm not talking houses.

Michael twists a finger around his bottle's neck. "Not much time." Oh yeah. Michael has to work to pay rent to his idiot dad.

"Moshie says you could have as many commissions as you can handle. You shouldn't be fixing cars."

"I know."

"I could watch Richie on your afternoons off." Richie is Michael's younger brother. He's so cute, but too quiet. Sort of like how Michael is around his dad. It's as though they're afraid to talk or think.

"No!" Michael's fierce, but not angry. He grasps my hand as though to pull it out of the fire. "You're not going there."

Given the tension in his "home," I'm glad he rejects this possibility. I can't imagine explaining to his dad that I'm watching Richie so Michael can paint. "Bring Richie to my house," I say.

He relaxes but doesn't say anything. He waits for me to admit this won't work, either. My parents would never let Richie or Michael come over. They want me to break up with Michael and stay away from his "disreputable friends." They can't wait for me to go off to college. I sigh. What will happen to Michael when I leave?

Michael misinterprets my sigh. "I'll finish it," he says. "Dad's hunting tomorrow, and I have the early shift at the garage, so Richie and I will be alone all afternoon. I'll paint then."

I long for summer, when he can take his paints, brushes, and canvases into the woods and spend hours working on a still life or a landscape. Planning to raise a hunter, not an artist, his dad taught him to slip through the forest like a shadow, so he paints wild animals when he finds them. But for two-thirds of the year, it's too cold to hold a brush in an ungloved hand, so he doesn't paint as much. Sometimes, when he or I have a car, we sneak over to Moshie's and he works. I hang with him, not saying much and reading whatever Moshie has around. I wish Michael were still in school. Mrs. Winthrop has added a bunch of new art classes he'd love. I give him the notes, but it's not the same as taking the class.

Andy has left center stage and is working the room, hitting on the girls and insulting the guys. Victor's gone into hiding with his own personal cooler. Josh is huddled by the fire, his hands clasped in front of him and his eyes following someone's movements. So, what do you know! Josh Stedman, priest in training, has the hots for a girl. I'm on the verge of telling Michael when Josh raises his head, and I see his face. I swallow my words. Then Michael nuzzles my neck as the wine cooler tops off my bladder. His kiss and the urge to pee converge in an idea, and I go upstairs like I have no other plan than to use the bathroom. Once upstairs, I find an empty bedroom, slip inside, and check the lock. It works.

From the top of the stairs, I watch Michael sitting by the fire. A couple has taken over most of the couch, and they're making out. He squeezes his lean body into a small space, as though he doesn't know what else to do besides give them room. He looks so alone. Maybe that's why I love him. We're both loners at heart.

When he sees me, I motion for him to come up. He saunters through the crowd, grabs a beer and a wine cooler, then heads for me. His black, curly hair bounces with each step. His tie-dyed QUESTION EVERYTHING shirt from Moshie's shop rises and falls rhythmically. Someone else might have thought he didn't care that I'd called him to make love. Someone else would've missed the way the bottles chattered in his artist's hands like a pair of fourth-grade girls'. Someone else wouldn't have seen the depth of the love in his eyes or the crinkle in his cheek where his dimple hides. But I did.

When he reaches the top, he takes my arm in his free hand and kisses me. Then he tries to hurry us out of sight. He doesn't want anyone to spread rumors that will reach my mother.

But I don't care. I stop and kiss him long and slow, like in the movies. *I claim this man,* I think. *I love him, and we'll be together always.*

Let the gossip begin. I'm ready for it. My parents can lecture me all they want about my supposed recklessness. I love Michael, and that's all that counts.

1

JOSHUA

CONFITEOR:
(Kneel)

"What's he doing with that?" I mutter as Andy pulls his dad's gun from the closet and admires the soft gleam of metal and wood in the dim light of the fire. Only three of us, Andy, Victor, and myself, are left in the cabin. I'm glad the party's over. I'm tired of being Andy's cleanup crew. Until he dragged out the gun, I'd actually been relaxing, something I don't do since my sister's accident. Mom told me to go out, insisting that Angela was okay. But she didn't mean for me to go to a drinking party.

Victor smirks. "Look. Andy's showing off. How unusual. Hell, he'd pull his main gun out of his pants to prove he has the best pecker. That is, if he didn't know he doesn't have anything on me there." I cringe as an image of us lining up for a penis-measuring contest pops into my mind. Not that it would happen with Andy or Victor. Neither would risk losing.

But Andy's unfazed. "Keep talking, Munger. You aren't bothering me." Andy sits on the couch and balances the gun on his lap. He bends his head and runs a finger over the wood. His light brown hair bleaches, then darkens as the flames flicker then gutter.

"Won't your dad be mad if you mess with his gun?" I ask, trying to keep my voice steady despite my growing nervousness. I don't want Andy to focus on me. Not when he has a gun and has been drinking. If I were smart, I'd have kept my mouth shut, but I wanted to defuse Victor's obnoxiousness.

Andy says, "What he doesn't know won't hurt him. He won't notice if I look at it." He smiles and strokes the wood as though it might caress him back. He has that tendency, to look for comfort in material things. Father Paul says solace can't be found in possessions, but I don't say that to Andy. Whenever I mention Father Paul, he jerks the conversation back to the world he knows, which isn't about peace and doing the right thing. It's about taking from and hurting others before they hurt you.

Sarcasm falls from Victor's lips like rain drops off a branch. "Your old man wouldn't notice anything that doesn't have a pussy."

Andy swings the rifle so fast, Victor doesn't have time to duck. The barrel strikes him hard in the chest and knocks him off his footstool. Andy has the gun cradled in his lap again before Munger has finished falling.

Victor climbs back onto the stool and rubs his chest through a thin T-shirt. His eyes are narrow. I've seen that look in gym class, right before he pulls an illegal move on someone who took his favorite parking place. "You're sure edgy, Andy, my boy." His tone is jovial, as if he's some church elder chastising an altar boy for an improper candlelighting technique, but his threat is there. I hope Andy controls his temper. "Everyone's gone now. Why don't you light some weed and mellow out?"

Typical of Victor to challenge Andy to do something really illegal. All night Andy's been making sure nothing happens that'll clue his dad in that the party took place. Calling him on this makes Andy look weak, or at least Victor thinks so.

"No pot," Andy says. "My dad'll smell it when he comes to close the pool tomorrow."

"His nose's that good?" Victor shifts away from Andy. The smack with the rifle hurt more than he wants to admit. His eyes follow Andy's hands, watching for movement or maybe an opening.

I shake my head. "Don't bug Andy." I've said it a thousand times to just about every kid in school. "Leave him alone." I ought to know. Andy's been my neighbor and friend since we were babies. His fuse is nonexistent, and he explodes without warning, like pure nitroglycerin.

Victor Munger isn't the best friend for Andy. He's too high-strung to steady him, and neither one talks. They hit. Of course, Andy has reasons for his anger. Always did have, but since his parents split up, his excuse list has gotten a lot longer. The only reason Victor has for his meanness is that he's a frickin' reptile with no heart. On top of that, his sex drive's always on high, and he has a nasty temper to rev up the Fahrenheit. Victor's fuse may be a mile long, but the stockpile of dynamite at the end is massive.

But I could always calm Andy—at least until a week ago, when I did the unforgivable. I asked Maggie out, which lost me Andy's respect. I don't know what's so bad about Maggie, other than she goes to church, sings in the choir, and is president of our youth group. He says the church's eating my brain. He was happy I was seeing someone, just not Maggie. "What'd you want to go out with that twig for anyway?" he whined when I said I couldn't go drinking with him. "She doesn't even have an ass. If you bounce her, you're going to get bruised up."

The thing is, I'm not going to bounce Maggie. I'm not going to bounce anybody. I'm not sure why I went out with Maggie. Dating a girl isn't exactly holding up my end of the deal. Maybe I had to test myself. She thinks so much like me and doesn't look down on me like Andy does because I pray.

Andy's pointing that damn rifle all over the cabin, and if I don't pull him up by the hair, he'll kill someone. First he aims at the refrigerator, like he's hunting dinner. Then at the stuffed trout on the wall. Then at the circular window in the peak of the cathedral ceiling. Then at the pillow by my feet.

My face goes hot as the gun moves from the pillow to my kneecaps. "Cut the crap, Andy. That thing better not be loaded."

Victor, his eyes heavily lidded, says, "Josh's right, you know. Cut the crap." He swigs his beer.

Andy inches the gun higher. "It's not loaded," he says as he points the gun at my chest.

I try not to show my fear, but I don't like guns. Unlike most everyone I know, I don't hunt. It's not just the killing, it's the gutting afterward. The sticky blood and foul intestines make me vomit. Not that I've said that to anyone. Most of my friends have guns, and the ones who don't have their own use their dads' guns to hunt. "Andy, put it down." My voice wavers, but Andy's hands don't.

"I said it isn't loaded." He squints as he sights down the barrel.

A door opens upstairs.

"Just like we're alone in the house. I thought you said everyone left!" Victor growls.

"Must be some late-night lovers," Andy says, his expression lewd. He flips the rifle barrel up like he's coming to attention or something, but it slams onto his shoulder so hard it jars his body. The gun explodes into the air behind his head. Not braced for the kick, Andy falls off his chair. He hits the floor, and the gun clatters onto the hard wood beside him.

A second later, I'm on my feet. Victor's frozen, head tilted back, a curious smirk on his face.

"Oh my God! Andy, are you okay?" I scream. I reach to help him up, not daring to look up at what Victor's staring at.

"Shut up, Josh! I'm fine," Andy says. He shakes his head, one hand pressed against his ear. "I'm deaf, I swear to the God that doesn't exist. Where's my beer?" He glares at the coffee table, which is littered with cans.

My eyes follow his. I will not look up.

Victor slaps Andy so hard across the head that I feel it. He points at the top of the stairs. I will not look up. I will not give this horror reality.

I remember the soft click of the door before the big bang of the gun. I moan. Time slows, then stops. I fall to my knees, will a prayer to my lips. Finally, I look up, and my eyes latch on to the nightmare.

Andy cries out, forgetting to be cool for one shocked

moment. Victor only snorts in accusation and disgust. I wail senseless words to God. Victor whacks my head hard, and I fall.

Death crouches above us, quiet, bewildered, unbelieving. The fire crackles, and a log settles. Death wears a blue sweater and has masses of tangled blond hair. But something's wrong with her sweater. It's changing to a reddish brown, starting in the center of her stomach and blooming outward. She huddles, mouth open but soundless as she sinks farther and farther toward the steps. Then she sits, her legs scrabbling out from under her. Her eyes at first hold stunned incredulity, then a sad certainty. Finally, with a sliding slump that pitches her down the stairs, they hold nothing.

Even a nonhunter like me knows the dullness of her eyes and the angle of her head mean only one thing. I close my eyes slowly, blotting the image from my sight if not my heart. Words scatter through my brain, but none bring help. My world, deal or no deal, God or no God, is over.

"You idiot!" hisses Victor, stepping forward. Time thaws, flows again. Victor's fuse crackles into life. We'll never put it out. He'll probably kill us both. His eyes have almost vanished into angry slits as he faces us, the cowards who aren't even checking on her. It's too new, too unbelievable. "It's Helen Mitchell. Our homecoming queen!" he spits at Andy.

Andy snickers. It's unavoidable. Does it matter what she was or wasn't? She's nothing now. A moment later, Andy's on the verge of tears. "Is she—?" he chokes, but he can't say it.

For an answer, Victor nudges her arm with his foot. "Yeah, she's dead. And if she's here, so is the scumbag she's messed up with." He stalks up the stairs like a panther on the hunt.

He doesn't notice that his padding feet step in smeared blood.

Without thinking, I raise a hand to stop him. Victor pauses, glances at me, then comes back down.

"Yeah, right. He doesn't need to know about this yet. He's probably smashed out of his mind anyway."

Which isn't what I'd been thinking. I'd been praying for a way to undo this, to go back to a minute ago, before the gun went off. And I'd been wishing Victor hadn't stepped in the blood. We had to call the police, and the less we disturbed things, the easier it would be to explain what happened. But the thought of explaining twists my guts. How can I tell Mom about this? What will I say to Helen's mother? Nothing comes to mind—except who will comfort me?

I turn to Andy like I've done every other time he's gotten us in trouble, and, like every other time, his brain is working, running, panicking behind his eyes. But whatever he's thinking won't fix this mess.

I glance at Victor and shudder. A scheme is growing in his mind, but from his tense, almost gleeful look, I know I won't like it. I dig deep, thinking through the 911 call I have to make, and I look at Andy. He won't go along with Victor. He'll do the right thing. Won't he?

"Michael has to be asleep, or he'd be down here already," Andy says. He's regaining some of his cool, but he keeps putting a hand to his ear and turning his head to catch every sound. "What do we do? Call the police?"

I relax, but before I can answer, Victor spins on him. "We? *We* don't do anything, stupid. *You* do. You wait until we're gone, then you call the police. I can't be mixed up with this. No way.

My old man, not to mention the long arm of Judge Johnson, will bust my ass for good."

"No—" I moan, but they don't hear me. I am caught, caged, strangled. "We all have to—"

It's almost as if I don't matter. Andy's not listening. Victor never would.

"You can't go anywhere," Andy says to Victor. He points at Victor's pant legs. "You're covered in evidence."

Victor follows Andy's pointing finger and cocks his leg to see what Andy's talking about. "Shit!" Blood has soaked his pant hem. The blood of a murdered girl.

I glance from Victor's narrowed, angry eyes to Andy, who's chewing his lip and plotting. I open my mouth to tell him again to call the police, but Andy moves toward Helen, crouches, and stares as though he's counting points on a buck's antlers. The slight glimpse I have of Helen's hand, lying in the pool of blood, makes me feel disemboweled.

I lose it. I run past them—dead girl and arguing guys—and rip into the fall night, my heaves twisting me inside out. Her eyes accuse me, beg me for help. But, oddly, there was no pain in her face, only shock, then certainty. Why hadn't she screamed? I puke soda and chips into the decaying leaves. Why had she stayed quiet? Had it happened too fast?

I throw my head back and stare at a branch-divided sky, wishing I'd driven so I could leave. I could call the police from a pay phone. I don't have to stay and be a part of Andy's plan. I'm not covered in blood. I did nothing wrong. Right? I was in the crosshairs of Andy's gun, too. It's pure dumb luck the gun didn't fire when he pointed it at me.

Dumb luck. I buckle again, bringing up the remnants of the pizza we had for supper. Then I cough up yellow bile that clings to my lips and teeth and tongue and makes me wish I could stick my head in a bucket of water and wash everything away. I stagger to my feet to find the Grabbits' pool, but Andy's in the doorway.

"Hey, Saint Josh! When you're done decorating the lawn, bring in one of the tarps covering the four-wheelers."

"Why?"

"Just do it!" The tough man is back in Andy's body. His uncertainty is gone. I have enough indecisiveness for both of us. I also have the only moral compass. Can I talk him into doing the right thing?

"Josh! I said, get the tarp!"

"Which one?" Stalling isn't working, not even for me. My legs have stood up, and without realizing it, I've taken several steps toward Andy. Habits of submission are hard to break.

"Any one! Does it matter?" He vanishes through the kitchen door, the one the bear supposedly came through. After a moment, Andy's head reappears.

Come out, Andy, I think, *before it's you dead on the floor. You can still make things right. Come on!*

"Better yet," he says, "make it a newer one. That way we can replace it easier."

"Replace it?" Something tears and collapses inside me. I'm shaking Jell-O in Andy's hands.

"Hey, Echo Man, can you move it? And when you have the tarp, get Dad's biggest four-wheeler ready, the one with the grille on the back. Make sure it runs."

"Why?"

"Shut up and do it!"

I jerk toward the garage. Andy isn't messing around. If he could reach me, he'd flatten me. He's punched the air out of me more than once when I argued with him.

Survival instinct sets in—that or shock—and I haul the newest-looking tarp off the biggest four-wheeler. My brain revolves around stupid details, like that Andy must have been in the garage earlier or it'd be locked. Either that or else it's dumb luck that it's open.

There it is again, damn it. Nothing is dumb luck. Luck means there's no God, and I never bought into that crap. My mind skitters off onto apes and molecules and chemical reactions—anything but what's really happening.

I run to the cabin with the tarp twined around my legs. I only fall once, which is amazing given how uncoordinated I am. Andy grabs the tarp and points behind me. I glare at him, but he only jabs a finger into my chest and says, "Do it! No questions."

I spin around like his finger is a cattle prod and fall down the back porch's steps. Behind me Andy mutters, "Christ, I'm surrounded by idiots."

Which is when I realize that Munger's screaming about Rosenberry's tree farm. When he appears behind Andy in the door frame, he tells Andy to think of a less populated route there. His voice is hard, cold as glacial rock. I can't see his face, but I can read his body language. Victor's not shaking and bent like me. He's not holding himself taut like Andy. He's easy in the hips and the back, and his head tilts like he's working through a math problem. He points a long finger at Andy and says, "I don't want to be caught cruising the woods with a body strapped on the back of your four-wheeler." He drapes an arm on Andy's shoulders and grins at me.

Andy stiffens like someone resolving not to give in, and for a second, I think he's decided to do what's right.

With Victor standing there like evil incarnate, their plan clicks and a cosmic *no* rises in me. For a moment, I'm calm. "What the hell are you thinking of doing, Andy? You have to call the police. You can't dump her." I look him straight in the eye.

But Andy has reinforcements now. And his reinforcement glares at me, mouthing threats, while Andy says, "Like hell I can't. You see that gun? I'll dump two bodies tonight if you don't do what I say. And if you even think of telling later, you stupid holy cow pie, I'll blow your whole family away. I didn't mean to kill her, but I'm not going to ruin my life by confessing to something that will get me locked up when I should be in college screwing girls. You got that?" Victor gives him a way-to-go shake.

He's got it all wrong, I think. *Can I make it to a phone?* But I say, "You don't want to go to jail, and I have to do what you say or you'll kill my family. Got it." Whatever Victor told him while I was puking, Andy thinks he has to do this to save his ass, even if it means killing me.

Victor gives him another little shake, then disappears into the cabin. Andy drops his voice. He's growling, low and threatening, like a cornered wolf. "Put your lip back in your mouth and get the four-wheeler. I can't believe you're being sarcastic now."

"And I can't believe you'd—" But it's no use. He cuts in and overrides my protest, which never should have included the word *believe*. He can say it, but not me.

"We're not discussing your beliefs here, man. How are you going to tell your parents that you were part of a threesome that killed a girl while drinking? What about your pillar-of-the-church grandma? You going to tell her you were partying, and oh, by the way, we shot a girl? I don't think so. Go start the machine."

I stand a moment longer, but I see Maggie, then Mom and Gram clutching each other while I'm handcuffed and led away. Funny that I think of Maggie first, since we've only been on one date. Funnier still that I'm standing here thinking of her while Helen is dead inside.

But where's Michael? I jump at a bang, thinking maybe he's woken and is raging against his girlfriend's murderers, but he hasn't. It's only Andy slamming the door behind him.

With leaden legs I return to the garage, where I search briefly for a phone, then start the largest four-wheeler. Maybe I'll have a chance to call 911 inside. Someone must have a cell phone. But something about the way Victor looked at me tells me that if I'm caught, it will be the last call I make.

2

MICHAEL

TAO TE CHING:

67

"If it is bent,

it will be preserved intact; . . ."

"Michael! Hey man, sorry about Helen. You should have known something would give and it'd be you."

I rub my head and look at Victor Munger. What's he doing here? Where's Helen? I peer around the bedroom in the dim light.

He stuffs something in his pocket, then produces a bottle of Hot Damn!. Two cups sit on the dresser across the room. He pours some liquor in one and hands it to me.

"What're you talking about?" I stifle a yawn and start to push myself up, then stop. I'm not wearing anything, so I stay half reclining.

"Helen! She skipped out on you! Some guy from downstate crashed the party and picked her up. They left together. You were pretty damn drunk, fighting and swearing, so we put you to bed." He blinks, as though that will make what he says easier to hear.

"She didn't leave with another guy. We—"

"Drink something," Victor says. "Then talk about it."

I raise the cup to my lips. True, her father has been riding her harder than usual lately, what with this being her senior year and me being two years older and blue-collar. But yesterday she'd promised to stick by me.

So why is Victor telling me that she's run off with some other guy? I swish the burning alcohol around my mouth for a second to kill the taste of beer and sleep, then turn to argue.

He's watching me, eyes narrowed like a cat that doesn't trust you. "You been fighting a lot with her folks lately?"

I nod, finding it harder and harder to remember. Behind him, someone moves. Then the door opens. The lights are on down-stairs. "Party still going?" I say, then feel the world shift.

"Going all night, pal. You finished with that?"

I stare at the full cup. I could've sworn it was empty a second ago. "Almost," I say, then pour the rest down my throat. I gasp.

"Wimp," Victor growls. "Pleasant dreams."

He doesn't wait for me to answer. Just walks out. I'm on my back by then, wondering why Helen would leave me after what we've been through. A tear slides down my face. I reach to wipe it away, but my hand never makes it.

3

JOSHUA

"I confess to almighty God, . . ."

I open my eyes to a blinding light and know I'm in hell.

Then I think, *I'm home, and it's time for Angela to be turned.* The hall light's on, and when I manage to ease my head into a different position, I see it's only 4:00 a.m. Time doesn't matter in hell. I'm in my room, and nothing's wrong.

But something happened. I have a muddled vision of riding on the handlebars of a four-wheeler with Victor screaming obscenities if I so much as turned my head. He had a knife stuck in his belt. He'd made sure I'd seen it before telling me to climb on. Then he'd told me to do what I was told and everything would be all right. The night had been quiet, except for us, and I wasn't contributing to the noise. *Let someone catch us before they do this, and I promise I'll never see Maggie again.* It'd worked before, why not now?

I sit up slowly. "Sorry," Mom murmurs, peering around the curtain that separates my side of the room from Angela's. "I didn't mean to wake you."

"It's okay. Do you need help?"

"No. Was the party fun?"

Why is she asking that? What's she looking at? My eyes skitter around the room like a puppy in a new place. I check for signs of dirt, blood, or blond hairs. I'm still wearing my pants, but I left my shirt with Victor. Unbelievably, he's the most skilled at laundry, as well as the one least likely to be caught. I can do laundry, but I can't bring bloody clothing home without causing a scene. He can do anything he damn well pleases, and we know it. But he reminded us in case we forgot. "Stupid wimps, letting old bags rule your lives," he'd said. "When you going to be a man, Stedman?" He didn't ask Andy anything because Andy was curled on the couch in the fetal position. He was crying. But we didn't comment on that because the gun was lying, uncleaned and still loaded, under him.

"Josh?" Mom says, worried. "You weren't drinking, were you? I mean, you didn't drive, but still you shouldn't drink." Her voice is soft, cautious. If Dad wakes up, he won't be able to go back to sleep. He'll wander the house, taking pictures off the walls. He won't explain why he's doing it, and his eyes will be flat, lifeless. No, it's much better to let him sleep, even if that's all he ever does when he's home.

Some stupid part of me hopes that the miracle I bargained for will include him getting better, but so far, no luck. "I'm okay," I say, "and no, I didn't drink. But you know Andy."

"You're only tired? Nothing unusual happened?"

Acid boils in my stomach. "Naw. We went to Mr. Grabbit's hunting cabin. Pretty boring stuff. They had some beer, I'm not going to lie, but nothing happened." My throat closes on "nothing," and a belch rises in my stomach, threatening to undo everything I've said. Nothing happened? Helen's dead! God only knows if Andy pulled himself together enough to clean the gun. Victor said it was the only thing left to do to make sure they couldn't pin it on us. That and keep our mouths shut about what happened. He'd said the last part with his hand on his knife.

Since I helped hide the body, I can't claim innocence.

Michael was plastered beyond recognition upstairs. I've never seen a guy on the date-rape drug, but he acted pretty much like I'd expected. Andy and I took a drugged girl home once. Andy said then, "I find my girls fair and square. This drugged-up shit is for wimps, perverts, and assholes." But he didn't comment when Victor pulled some of the drug from his wallet and suggested giving it to Michael. Just nodded and poured another slug of whiskey down his throat.

Mom strokes my head and then pulls the sheet up on Angela. Angela gurgles, but if she's awake, her eyes aren't open. Her hair, I realize with a jerk, is the same shade of gold as Helen's.

I make this little choking sound, and Mom swings back to me, her eyes sharp in the light from the doorway. I turn away, trying not to see her questions, only feeling the pain of knowing that she's doubting me, which she's never done before. I force myself to lie back, to close my eyes, even though when I do, I see Helen's body, partially wrapped in blue tarp, lying beside the ragged hole Andy and Victor dug. I see Victor shove her in, and I watch her hair slither over the dirt and rocks.

I roll onto my side and face the wall so I can open my eyes without Mom knowing. Even after she goes back to bed, I don't sleep.

Guilt works like a plunger on my guts. I run for the bathroom to puke air and spit and dangling slime until I collapse on the linoleum. I shake with sobs until the alarm goes off at eight.

It's Sunday. The day of rest. The holiest day of the week. The first day without Helen on earth in approximately seventeen years. I deserve God's wrath for what I've done. So far, though, God hasn't noticed my sin. I'm alone with my guilt.

I crawl into the tub, turn the water on high, and think of drowning myself. But with Angela's accident, there's been enough of that in our family. I end up shampooing my hair like nothing's wrong.

4

MICHAEL

*"[If it] is crooked,
it will be straightened; . . ."*

My head feels like it's been cut off and stuck in a freezer. My nose is stuffed, and my throat's raw. The squelch of tires and the roar of cars on a main road rush into the room. What road?

Lifting my head makes lights explode. Pushing my body up causes the world to evaporate in a swirl of threatening and disorienting colors. What the hell did I drink last night, and where the hell am I? Where's Helen?

Helen! I bolt upright, face the sweep of black that washes over my vision, then shake my head to clear it. "Helen?" I croak, putting a hand to my throat. The shades are drawn, and I don't remember doing that. Hell, I don't remember last night. I only remember Helen, that she'd had a massive fight with her dad, and she'd had to sneak to see me. Where had we gone? Where was I?

I shove a foot toward the floor, then swing the other after it. It takes thought and planning to stand, but as I stagger to the window, I trip on something that skitters away. I stumble the remaining two steps and yank the shades, guarding my eyes with my hand. When I can see, I glance at the bed. No Helen. I look at the floor to find what I tripped on. I freeze.

It's a gun. New, glinting, oiled, and polished. Unused? I bend partway down, then think better of it. I crouch and touch the wooden stock. I whistle. Dad would kill for a gun as pretty as this one. I've listened to his endless lectures on how to corner your prey. He taught me how to walk the woods with the stealth of a cat. I know guns, and this is a beaut. I pick it up and check to make sure the safety's on. It's not. I crack it. One round's missing. Out of habit, I pop the remaining shell and set it on the tall dresser. I put the safety on and lean the gun against the wall behind the door.

I glance around. This is Andy Grabbit's cabin, but the gun's owner could've been anyone at the party. Half the town was here, drinking, showing off, pairing off. Who would mess with a gun at a party?

Does it matter?

I find the bathroom and my clothes, not in that order, because you never know who'll be left when you wake up after a party. Then I search for Helen.

The place is remarkably clean, given last night's wildness. Then again, I wouldn't mess with Mr. Grabbit. I'm probably more leery of him than my own dad, and he's nothing to sneeze at.

But I don't care about them. I want to find Helen. For some reason, I think she left with someone, but I've no idea why. I search the cabin but find no sign of her or anyone else.

In the bedroom where I woke, I pull back the blankets because I have these dueling memories. I can feel, taste, see Helen with me, kissing, touching, laughing. But then there's this other memory that's all words, and not in Helen's voice. Someone told me she left, that we fought.

But there, on the sheet, is the proof that my first memory is real. We were here together. We made love.

I yank the blankets over the stain, then look for anything, some evidence to prove that I'm not insane. I find it under the big dresser, although I have no reason to look there. It's a sock. Helen always wears these funny socks with pictures on them—flowers, dogs, weird old women, hats, scarves, circles, and dots. This one is black with neon cats arching and hissing on it. No way is it someone else's. "Helen?" I say into the stillness.

No answer.

That's when I check the time. Two in the afternoon? Holy shit. My ass is grass, and it'll be mowed if I don't get out of here. Everyone knows Mr. Grabbit is closing his pool today, which is why we were supposed to pee in it last night. I didn't. But Dad's home, waiting for me to watch Richie so he can go turkey hunting. Ever since I quit hunting, I have to babysit.

I blow out of there like the cops are after me, Helen all but forgotten, her sock stuffed in my jeans pocket.

5

JOSHUA

". . . and to you, my brothers and sisters, . . ."

When I come out of the bathroom, I collapse on my bed, certain Mom won't be in to turn Angela for at least an hour. I reach for my Bible. I want to be told what to do, how to deal with this, but my hand closes over a slimmer book. On the cover, a wolf's face challenges me with steely eyes and a condescending expression. Angela's journal is one of those cardboard books with a stupid, cheap lock. These locks are so easy to pick, and the strap holding it shut is only vinyl. They can't keep a nosy brother out.

But I've never violated Angela's diary. Angela was supposed to come back. I bargained with God to make sure that happened. But what kind of miracle did God do? Angela returned, but she's as broken as this lock will be in a minute. I hesitate, surprised at my thoughts, but no all-forgiving love envelops me. Only silence. I slide a pen under the little strap and pull. It stretches but doesn't break. Sort of like me.

Did last night nullify my vows?

I'd tried to call the police. I went to use the phone in the kitchen while Victor was busy with Michael upstairs. I planned on hiding in the pantry and muttering my statement. But the cord connecting the receiver to the phone was missing. Victor had anticipated me like some sort of prescient monster.

Andy caught me turning away from the phone.

My face must've looked comical, I was so shocked and disappointed.

Andy didn't smile. He sucked in a big nicotine rush and blew it at me in a long hiss. "Thanks, buddy. Now I owe Victor one beer," he said. He lowered his gaze to the fire. "When I owe him a six-pack, I have to kill you. Nothing personal. We can't afford the risk." He rubbed his hands on his pants. His eyes flew from the fire and stopped when they hooked mine. "I don't want to kill you, Josh. We go back too far, so don't mess up." He looked away.

I collapsed onto the couch and didn't move. I remember thinking how very important it was to stay still. That must be how a mouse feels when the grass rustles nearby, how a deer feels when it catches the scent of man or hears his heavy tread. *Don't move. The danger will pass.*

Maybe Andy could earn a beer back from Victor if I acted right. Then I wouldn't be on death's path. But I knew there was nothing I could do to warrant that. No matter what, I couldn't win.

I shivered. This wasn't a game. If I was weak, I'd be in that hole with Helen. Maybe it was the tone of Andy's voice as he begged me not to mess up. Maybe it was Andy's gun that convinced me. It lay on the floor, loaded and within easy reach.

Was this the purpose of my life? To be a witness to life's sense-lessness and man's cowardliness?

Andy glared at the fire's embers like they might leap from the grate and attack him. Could I make him see reason? But I'd only drawn breath before he said, "Shut up, Josh. I'm not in the mood to hear preaching."

I shifted. "We don't have to—"

His fist caught me in the chest. "We do!" he shouted as I fell off the couch. "Oh yeah, we do!"

I picked myself off the floor.

But I never recovered. If I had, I wouldn't be picking my sis-ter's diary lock right now. The strap's tougher than I expected, so I pilfer a long needle from the red plastic medical waste bin that hangs by Angela's bed, and I cram it into the lock. It grates and scrapes. Then it snaps to the left with a click.

What am I doing? What if Angela saw me? But she won't. Not now, maybe never. What if she dies? She'd go to heaven, and I wouldn't have known her.

I flip to a random page. My eyes bug with anticipation, then with surprise, then disgust.

I fling the diary onto the softness of my bed, careful even in anger not to disturb Mom or Dad.

After a moment, I cradle the diary and reopen it. Page after page mocks me. In a house with little privacy and only flimsy locks, Angela had erected a wall around her heart. She wrote her diary in code. Probably not a complicated one, but one that speaks volumes of what she thought of me, Dad, and Mom. She hadn't trusted us.

I close the diary, try to jam the lock shut again, but it's broken.

The strap flaps open, useless. I almost laugh as it dangles like a tooth hanging by a thread in a five-year-old's mouth. Then I choke on my fear. I don't have time to break Angela's code, translate a diary, and discover my sister before she comes back.

She *will* come back. She has to. I want to ask her what's on the other side of life. I want to know what kind of God allows an innocent girl to die and another to be held prisoner in a decaying body. Angela's the only person who can answer my questions. Not even Father Paul knows. So she has to come back.

I slip the diary under my bed as Mom rushes in, panicked because she overslept.

"I turned her," I call just loud enough for her to hear. "Relax. She's okay."

Angela gurgles, chokes, resumes breathing. Mom suctions her tube, fusses with her blankets, then nods as though her duty is done. As long as Angela lives, though, Mom's duty will continue.

Mom faces me. Her hands smooth her hair, pat her robe into place. "Thank you, Josh. What do you want for breakfast?"

Angela's eyes are open. They stare through me, reading what I did, knowing my sin.

I gag, cover my mouth, gag again.

Angela's eyes close.

Mom says, "Josh? Are you okay? Maybe breakfast will settle your stomach?"

So she believes I've been drinking. But I don't need my stomach "settled." Nothing short of a miracle will ever calm my stomach again.

6

MICHAEL

"[If it] is sunken,
it will be filled; . . ."

He's sitting in his chair on the side of the room that counts as living space. The dining-room table is piled with his gun, license, shells, boots, and camouflage jacket, pants, and hat. He doesn't turn as I come in. The clock pulses its way to three. He says, "Pretty damn useless going hunting an hour before sunset."

It's at least three hours before sunset, but I don't say that. I stay quiet, looking into the narrow kitchen—spotless as always—for Richie, and for something I can grab to steady my stomach. There's nothing.

"Richard's in his room. Get your ass in there, too, and don't come out until I come home. I'll deal with you then." Now he's behind me, moving soft like the cat I've learned to imitate. I'm only an apprentice to the master, which my slight startle at his closeness reveals. His breath, hot and sour, puffs against my neck. I don't turn to see his smirk. "Don't think I won't remember." He backs off, already in his jacket.

I can't move past him. He's dressing in the door. His pants

slide up his legs as if they've been greased for silence. They probably have. Any advantage a hunter can claim is fair to Dad. His eyes are on his task, but his rage is on me. It's like a wall, pushing against me, trying to smother my resentment. At least he's silent.

He always senses my relief and makes his move then. "Two weeks, you shithead. You have two weeks to get your ass out of my house."

It's a threat as constant as the sun's rising and still as potent. He kicked me out twice before I graduated, when I couldn't support myself. Both times he took me back, mostly so I could watch Richie. He's threatened me again since I found a job, but I pay rent now, and he needs the money. But something's different in his voice today. Something that says he's not messing around.

He's dressed, and he shoves shells into his pocket. His turkey call follows, although he doesn't need it. He talks turkey so well he's never come home empty-handed. Just once, I wish he would. So he could feel disappointment in someone other than me. So he could see he's not perfect.

But if he comes back without his prey today, it'll be my fault. He'd missed the good hunting due to my lateness. A sigh swells my lungs, but I don't let it out. Never show your weakness.

He's at the door. In two more steps I can move, go see how Richie is, call Helen. But he stops. "Mr. Lydon called. You're fired." He's out the door fast, but not rushed. He never hurries. Why should God rush?

"Shit." I slide down the wall to huddle on the floor in defeat. I'd completely forgotten that I was scheduled to pump gas from six to twelve. I was also supposed to pound out that station wagon's left fender and take off the crumpled left doors. Mr. Lydon would've arrived to find nothing done and no money in the register. I can see his face, tight, red, pissed. I can hear his voice on the phone, the smug satisfaction that he could chuck another lazy kid. "Shit." I punch the wall, being careful not to leave a mark. Dad would know who did it.

A door opens down the hall, my door, Richie's door. His feet appear before I can arrange my face into a smile to greet the only thing besides Helen that's good in my life. "I didn't do it," Richie says. "I tried to stop him."

I stare at him, my world a blank. I may have lost Helen. I've lost my job. What could Dad do that would hurt me more? But from Richie's tight face and straining, swaying body, I know Dad managed to destroy the one thing I have left.

"I'm sorry, Michael. He found the spot. I didn't tell him. Honest." He's crying, tears dripping down his white face like melted wax.

"The spot." It could only mean one thing. I jump to my feet, and Richie darts aside. Our room is a mess and not because Richie and I are allowed to be slobs. The carpet is covered by a snow shower of white paper, none of it bigger than an inch square. Broken sticks with furry tails litter the floor. Trays, speckled with old paint, are twisted and rent apart. I turn to Richie. "My paintings? Helen's portrait?"

He shakes his head, and my hope plummets. I pull back the loose paneling and peer inside. Nothing.

I drop to my knees, searching the snippets for canvas or painted watercolor. I find only pencil sketches. I scramble to my desk, yank open drawers. No paintings.

Richie touches my shoulder, his deep brown eyes scared but earnest. "They're in his room."

I squeeze his hand. It's not his fault.

Dad's room. His locked room. But I'm not my father's son for nothing. The rage he gave me boils and overflows. I rush from our room like a linebacker taking out an opponent twice his size. His door is directly opposite ours. I smash it with my shoulder, and it splinters beneath my weight, thanks to cheap construction. What the hell does it matter that I broke it? Helen's gone, and her emptiness is everywhere. I've lost the last "position" the Job Center said they could find me, and the prick I call Dad has ruined my paintings.

They sit on his bed. A neat double row of landscapes and portraits. Each picture has a markered letter on them. Arranged as they are, his message is plain. Y-O-U S-T-U-P-I-D A-S-S-H-O-L-E. He expected me to break in! God, I hate him.

I gather the paintings with shaking hands. Helen has an O around her face, more in her hair than over her skin. Maybe I can fix her. But my supplies are destroyed. Everything's gone. I have money, and I know where he keeps his. I grab the cedar box from his closet, and Richie screams.

"Hush, Richie. You know I can't stay here. He kicked me out."

"He'll kill you if you take his money."

I clutch my paintings. "He already has." I flip open the box.

No You Don't is written on the top paper. I dig deeper. Nothing. Not even twenty bucks. The hundred dollars I paid him two days ago for rent isn't there, either. I throw the box at the wall, and it breaks into three pieces.

Richie whimpers. From somewhere inside me, Helen says, "You are not him. Don't let him win by making you into him." I shudder and stop. *Think!* I tell myself. *Richie first.*

He's crumpled in the doorway, his ten-year-old body convulsing in sobs. I sit beside him, force steadiness into my voice, and say, "I'll come back for you, I promise." But something tears inside me. Something flies off like a leaf in a windstorm. It's hope. How can I come back? What can I do against Dad? How can I beat him? One look at Richie's devastated face tells me I have to. I take him in my arms, make shushing noises, try to convince him, and therefore me, that I can rescue him.

"You can't leave me. Mom did, and now you are. I can't stay. I'll run away, I swear. I'll kill myself."

I swallow another sigh. "Stay low. I'll clean this up and our room, take what I can find of my own, then leave. He can't blame you. He won't." I don't say, *Not yet. Not while he can blame me.* "And you know your mom didn't leave you. He worked the courts, said she was unfit."

"He drove her crazy!"

"I know, Richie, I know. But she's better. She'll get you back. I'll testify. I'll tell them what it's like here. They'll give you to her, I'm sure of it." Why hadn't I fought harder, told more? My stomach twists away from the truth. I didn't do it so Richie had to stay with me. As though I could protect him from Dad. Now look what happened. I can't take him with me, I'm sure of that.

I'm also sure that if I went to Richie's mom's house and asked her for shelter, she'd give it. But Dad would look for me there. He'd kill her if she helped me, or he'd make sure she never saw Richie again. He'd run off with him, as he'd done with me, leaving a broken woman behind so he could find a whole one to destroy. Keep the son, toss the mother into the garbage.

If I had any guts, I'd turn him in for hunting on a Sunday, but he'd only be fined. He'd still be loose, able to hurt me, hurt Richie.

I had to be careful where I went, but I had to go. I rocked with Richie for a minute more, then I cleaned up. Dad's room had to be spotless when he came home. It had to be exactly as he left it, minus the door, the box, and my paintings. I couldn't fix the broken things, and I wouldn't leave my paintings. I rolled the paintings, one inside the other, and wrapped them in newspaper. I rubber-banded them into a tube, then tied the tube to my bag. Richie helped clean our room. His hands shook, and his eyes watched my every move. It took two hours to make it Dad-acceptable. Packing took five minutes.

Then I was out of there. I forced myself to turn and wave only once. If I did it any more, I'd run back, grab Richie, and take him with me. So I walked alone up our long rutted driveway, then down the dirt road to the paved one where I could hitch a ride.

That is, if no one recognized me. Anyone who knew me as Jeb Knight's son wouldn't stop. But the weekend hunters, fishermen, and other vacationers sometimes pulled over. It's one of these who picks me up. "Mind if I tag along?" I ask when he says he's going back to Pittsburgh.

He looks surprised.

"Lost my job here. Haven't been able to find another." I press my back against the seat and try to look respectable. "Thought I could find work in Pittsburgh."

He nods. He's about fifty, balding, paunch fully developed, but he has soft blue eyes, the kind that crinkle when he smiles. Which he does now. "Pretty much how I started in life," he says. "Took off to the big city one day and never looked back. Kept in touch, though." He glances at me.

I nod, recognizing his unspoken command. I'll keep in touch, all right. I'll always write Richie, but I mean to bring that s.o.b. low.

"I own two drugstores. Maybe—" He pauses to size me up.

I keep my oil-dirtied, paint-spotted hands curled tight around the straps of my backpack. I thank Helen, God, and even my dad's fanatical neatness that I look presentable. Helen had never let me get more than the one tattoo I already had when we met, and she'd asked me to let my eyebrow piercing grow over. I'd agreed, mostly because it was infected anyway, and it'd get Dad off my back without giving in to him. Now this guy gives me the okay, and I ease up in the shoulders.

He nods, and his eye crinkles reappear. "Maybe I can find something for you to do at one of them."

"I'd appreciate that, sir."

"Sir!" he says. "Mr. Lockwood will do. Tell me what your name is and a bit about yourself."

I tell him about Helen, about painting, about Richie. If he notices I don't mention a mother or a father, he says nothing. But a sadness creeps into those blue eyes, eyes I've already begun to like.

7

JOSHUA

". . . that I have sinned through my own fault . . ."

Mom can't go to Mass. She can't leave Angela, who hasn't left her bed for over a month, ever since her souped-up wheelchair was replaced by a respirator. Mom says I have to go for her, giving me that smile that says she'd love a break, even if it was to go to church. It's hard to find volunteers to care for Angela, and we can't afford to pay anyone. The spaghetti-dinner fund-raisers have long since stopped. Other people, other tragedies have taken the headlines from us, and with it, the public's help. If only one of us can go, she sends me. Maybe she's being a martyr, but I think she believes I need to go more than she does. I don't argue with her today, because I need to beg God's forgiveness and plead for His mercy.

I go to Mass alone. I can't ask Dad for the car since he's sleeping on the sofa. He'll pull himself together to go to work tomorrow, but until then, we won't bother him. It's just as well—I can't stand the emptiness of his eyes. Besides, I can ride my bike to town. I pass the remnants of a flower garden by the toolshed where my bike is stored, and I almost remember what normal is. Or was. We all used to go to church on Sundays. We'd say our prayers, and Angela and I would go to youth group and cate- chism. Mom was a lay minister. At home we'd garden, swim, or fish. In the winter, we'd shovel snow, chop wood, build snow- men, sled, or skate on the pond if it was frozen.

We rarely go near the pond now. Dad had stocked it with fish before; they must be huge by now. "Go forth and multiply," he'd said with a sly look at Mom. Too bad he's lost his sense of humor. It might have kept us normal, but what did I expect? How would I react to finding my daughter facedown in a pond?

I'm feeling easier toward him because the sun's shining and I think Angela smiled this morning. Gratitude for the little things is easier to feel when something big goes horribly wrong. Helen's death puts even Angela's condition in perspective. It's not what I asked for, but while she lives, I have hope. For Helen there is no hope. I start to shake, so I shove the thought of Helen to the back of my mind, close a door on it, and focus instead on the Psalms I've memorized.

I'm early, but the church's open. The curtains to the confes- sional are pulled back, but I can't go there. Images of Andy's gun and Victor's slitted eyes gleaming over his knife bar my path. I choose a pew in the inconspicuous middle of the church. I try to pray, but the words jumble and twist into screams I can't let out.

She didn't receive last rites or a decent burial, my heart argues.

Manslaughter, my head answers. That's what Victor'd said we'd get if the police found out. Because we helped dispose of her body.

But wasn't burying her body only tampering with evidence?

How much time do you do for that? Andy'd get manslaughter, sure. But me?

How much time will I serve in my prison of guilt? Pity settles on me like a heavy robe, then my gut wrenches. How can I pity myself when Helen's dead? Images flash through my brain like laser attacks: Helen's hair mixed with clotted earth. Her sweater darkened by blood and dirt. The thumps of dirt falling on the tarp, the scrapes of shovels gouging the earth. My empty stomach tears, buckles, revolts. Helen's mother smiling at a newborn.

What about her mother?

Mrs. Mitchell will be waiting for Helen to come home, her hands clutching ever tighter as the hours pass and she doesn't appear.

I jump up. The urge to tell, to relieve myself and everyone else of this terrible burden, strangles me.

Which is when I see Munger easing into my pew. I sit again, heart racing. He doesn't belong to our parish. He doesn't even believe in God. Why is he here?

He slides along the wooden bench until his thigh touches mine. I'm cold, then hot. Unspoken threats pass from his tense leg into my wobbling leg. He reaches for the missal, rips out a page, and, using the pencil provided for visitors to fill out cards, writes, You CONFESS, YOU DIE. SHE DIES.

My brain skitters like a stone skipped across water. *I could beg Father for sanctuary*, I think. But what "she" would Victor kill while I hid here? My eyes focus on the painted statue of Mary and Jesus. Angela. My breath flows out of my body like blood from a wound. I hear the *wush-wush-shup* noise the paper makes as it trembles in my hand. If I claim sanctuary—and after what

I've done, I don't have that right—I can't protect Angela. And I owe her that. Or does he mean he'll kill Mom?

Victor takes the paper from my hand and folds it, once, twice, three times, creasing each fold with a slide of his thumbnail that sounds like a knife being drawn. He leans back and shoves the folded note into his pocket, then drapes his arm behind me on the pew. He's not going anywhere. He's going to dog my steps, make my life miserable. He leans over and whispers, "You're the weakest link. I am not going to jail. I got into Penn State early admission, and I'm not giving that up because some stupid idiot shot a dumb blonde."

I want to scream that Helen wasn't dumb, she was nice, a good kid. She was in two of my classes, and Maggie was her friend.

Maggie! Is that who he meant to kill? What have I done?

I sit there. My heart knocks against my teeth. My knees shake the entire pew. I stare at the Cross. I'm in church, in His House, and I'm being threatened. Where is He?

After a minute, Victor stands. He drags his hand across my neck in what I'm sure looks friendly to the few people behind us, but his fingernails dig into my flesh.

I don't feel God at all.

8

MICHAEL

"[If it] is worn-out,
it will be renewed; . . ."

The next day, I take some money and buy a phone card and a few postcards. I know better than to call Helen's house. Her dad will hang up on me faster than he slams the door on Jehovah's Witnesses. I write a note on the first postcard, using Shelly's address, like I've done before. She'll pass it on to Helen.

> *Dear Helen,*
> *I'm okay. Dad kicked me out again, so I hitched a ride with this great guy who's given me a job in Pittsburgh. I miss you and wish you were here with me. He'd probably give you a job, too, but you need to finish school. Tell Mrs. Winthrop I'll buy her a new Picasso book. Dad ruined hers. I'll call soon at our normal time.*
>
> > *Love you always,*
> > *Michael*

I want to ask what happened, where she went and why, but don't. Even if she went with another guy, I wouldn't blame her. What do I have to offer her? Sure we fit like gloves, but maybe only I thought that. Maybe she decided that her parents are right. They claim they only want her to be happy, but they don't seem happy. They fight over dumb things, like who turned up the thermostat or why her dad ate the tortilla chips when he knew they were having company.

Helen and I don't fight. She has different opinions than I do, but I listen to her, and sometimes I agree. Like about the eyebrow bar and new tattoo. Moshie had told me the same things, but it was Helen I listened to.

Moshie. Could he send a message to Richie that I'm okay? It's worth a try. I dial the store, but forget it's Monday, Moshie's day off. The line clicks, then Moshie's sawdust voice croaks the store's hours. After the beep, I say, "Moshie, it's Michael. I'm okay. Can you call Richie—"

Another beep sounds, cutting me off. He doesn't leave much space for messages. Probably doesn't want them. Maybe idiots like Helen's dad call and leave angry messages, filling his voice mail, and he's sick of it. I never gave much thought to what Moshie goes through to give kids a place to be themselves.

I sigh. Maybe Helen will go there tomorrow, talk to Moshie, and learn that I'm okay. She knows my dad, and she's afraid of him. Seeing the guns in my house scared her. She's very anti-hunting. She thinks predators should be reintroduced to keep the deer population under control. She hates the newspaper photographs of coyotes strung up dead. "They're dogs!" she'd cried to me once, pointing to a photo. Proud men grinned and clutched guns behind their kills.

"Coyotes," I'd corrected, but she'd shaken her head to block out my explanation. "It's legal to shoot a coyote whenever you see one."

"They look like dogs to me. How can you tell that they didn't shoot their neighbors' mutts? They don't care about the coyote's role in the ecosystem." She'd jabbed a finger into the face of one of the hunters.

"Maybe not, but you grew up here. You hear them howling in the woods. All the farmers have stories of coyote attacking their herds."

"Myths, Michael. Those stories are myths."

I'd looked at her and seen the glistening of tears. I'd drawn her close. "Maybe they are, but I don't know. Find me a book that says otherwise, and I'll believe you. I'll be a new recruit for the Preserve the Coyote Association."

She'd wiped her eyes. "Oh, Michael, I'm serious."

"I am, too. Prove it to me. It'll be good practice for when you're running for office."

"I'll never do that."

"Well, you should."

"Why?"

"Because—" I'd stopped. Why would she be a good politician? "Because you care so much. You're so sincere and earnest. Besides, the camera loves you, and that's half the battle of being elected. And you're clean."

"Michael!" She'd swatted my arm.

"Clean as in drug-, alcohol-, and scandal-free."

"I don't know about that," she'd said, her eyes glinting with some secret joke. "I date you." She'd drawn out the word *date*, filling it with hidden meaning.

I'd ignored her.

"That's a scandal, isn't it?" She'd moved closer. We were alone at her house, studying, or rather she was supposed to be. I was there to read over her notes from art class. Mrs. Winthrop had added a bunch of classes, and I was trying to take them through Helen. But Helen didn't have homework or her political future in mind as she bent over me, her mouth open and inviting. "It's scandalous how she acted with that boy," she'd murmured before our lips met.

The only thing that could have ruined that moment did. Her mother arrived home, shouting Helen's name and hurrying through the house as though determined to catch us in action.

Helen had kissed me a last time, then drifted to her desk. When her mother thrust open the door like she'd expected to find us buck-naked and riding for heaven, we'd only looked up. "God, Mom. Don't you believe in knocking? We might have been doing something private, you know."

Mrs. Mitchell had given me a puzzled, frightened look, then said, "You shouldn't be studying up here. You know the rules."

Helen had pointed at her computer. "Researching on the Web. When Dad gets a computer downstairs, I'll do my work there."

"Watch your tone, Helen. You still live under our roof. We can make your life miserable." She'd fled after that.

Helen had waited for her footsteps to fade. "You already have," she'd said.

"Shhh," I'd warned. They could make it much worse if they wanted. But even with how nasty she was to me, I never thought Mrs. Mitchell hated me. She was scared of me, but I didn't know why.

They're probably celebrating my disappearance. "He left without a word to Helen. Now she knows what a creep he is."

I hope she knows I love her and that I'll call her as soon as I can.

9

JOSHUA

(Strike breast)

Maggie's standing with the usual group of girls by the refreshment table after church. She holds a soda, and her head tilts like she knows I'm watching her. Is she hoping I'll come over? We've only had one date, but for me to go that far was a big deal.

It broke my promise.

And now my promise is shattered, trampled, buried.

Did we bury her deep enough? Will someone find her? How soon?

I walk toward Maggie, my steps uneven. She smiles more broadly and flashes a look at her friends. They giggle and slip away.

She coughs, giggles, then says, "Hi, Josh," like she's been waiting for me to say something. Her black hair almost reaches her hips. At the movies, she'd wound it over her shoulder in a long coil. It'd fallen across my arm, resting like that the whole movie, caressing my skin and sending wild thoughts through me.

I unglue my eyes from her hair and say, "Hi." Brilliant. I force my mouth to say more. "What're you doing?"

"Youth group," she says. "The hayride's today. Are you going?"

Hayride? "When?"

"This afternoon. The Rosenberrys have loaned us their horses."

"The Rosenberrys have horses?" A black pit of panic gapes at my feet, and I sway.

"Duh. Their daughter shows them, remember? Are you feeling okay?"

"Yeah, fine," I lie. "I thought they ran a tree farm."

"Her dad does, but she's big on the 4-H thing, so they raise draft horses on the farm. Do you need a ride?"

I can't go there. They can't go there. Helen is there. I tremble, lurch into the pit, feel myself falling. The rush of air pushing past forces my breath from my lungs.

"Josh?"

I gasp and squeak out an excuse. "I rode my bike. I can't go."

"We could load it in the back of my dad's car. Come on, it'll be fun. Most of the guys are too macho to go. I was hoping you'd be different." She gives me that begging look I've known since first grade. But I force myself not to give in. How can I go on the same trails that I rode on last night?

She takes my hand.

If I could stare in her eyes forever, I could keep my promise to Victor.

But Maggie starts to look worried, because I've forgotten to answer her.

My lips form a tight smile. Misinterpreting it as a yes, Maggie drags me to the bike rack.

Like water balloons, my legs wobble. No way am I up to biking home. "I can't go on the ride, but you can drop me at my house before," I say.

She shakes her head no, grinning like she's won. "I can't. I don't have time. I'm in charge of the whole thing," she says. "I have to arrive early. Please? I'd like you to come."

I try to protest again, but she's talking so fast I can't cut in.

Two other girls already lean against her car. It takes five minutes of careful planning to squeeze my bike in the trunk, then I'm given the front seat and the girls take the back. Maggie lets out a whoop along with the emergency brake. Queen reverberates through the car, and the girls join the chorus. "Come on, Josh, sing," they scream. "'Another one bites the dust, and another one, and another one. . . .'"

I feign exhaustion, so Maggie turns down the music. The girls gossip the rest of the way, but I don't listen. I concentrate on keeping my mind empty until we pull up to the barn.

Dusty flakes of straw flutter in the air as I follow Maggie toward the wagon. Steam rises from a fresh plop of manure behind the horses. Angela, who had loved animals, would have been delighted to be here. And guys would have joined her. She attracted guys like cake attracts ants.

A hand reaches toward me. Maggie, already in the wagon, is offering to help me up because I'm standing lost in thought. I shake my head and grab the wooden slats. I climb a rickety step into the wagon, which sways with the shifting of the horses' haunches. Maggie steers me to a place on one of the side benches. Mr. Rosenberry, the driver, gives me a smile. "One guy, eleven girls—not a bad dating plan," he says. "If they drive you nuts, come up here with me."

Maggie's squashed against me, and her lilac-scented hair smothers the poop smell. I stay put.

"Did you hear—?"

"Did you hear—?"

The chorus of gossip, the song of conjecture circles me. My head starts to hurt.

Then a short girl who's in my English-comp class says, "Did you hear that Helen Mitchell never came home last night?"

I jerk, but Maggie's leaning over to contribute to the story, so she doesn't see. "Did her parents call yours? They called mine."

My mind spins in fear like a kaleidoscope, and the colors of the girls' sweaters—gold, green, red, and blue—tumble across my swirling vision.

"They called everyone's."

"His?"

"No one knows, but don't you think they did?"

"Probably."

"Anybody seen him?"

"The gas station wasn't open this morning."

Whistles and giggles and I-told-you-so looks.

My heart and breathing have stopped. I clutch my sweatshirt's hem to keep from clawing my eyes or plugging my ears.

"Shelly said they went to Andy's party, and Helen was there when she left."

Shelly could name every one of us. She knew who had stayed and who had gone. Unless she was too drunk to remember. I hope she was plastered. But she remembered that Helen was still there. If Victor could threaten me in church, what would he do to Shelly?

The wagon jolts forward, and Maggie falls against me. I go for a surefire topic change and put my arm around Maggie.

The girls don't notice, not even Maggie. Mr. Rosenberry does. His grin is almost lecherous as he checks to make sure none of us have fallen out. Eleven girls and one geeky guy making a move on his dreamboat. I drop my arm.

"Do you think they ran off together?"

"Why wouldn't they wait until she graduated?"

"Maybe she's pregnant, and they went to find a clinic that would do an abortion."

"Maybe he—"

"Maybe she—"

A scream presses against my tonsils; my head bangs like a steel drum; my legs shake from lack of food and sleep. The trail twists and turns. Rows of Christmas trees give way to fields of staked seedlings. These morph into scrubland that's more blackberries and burrs than trees, then into the forest. Mr. Rosenberry clucks his horses up a lumber trail that switchbacks up the hill.

Branches snap past my face, and the clinging whisper of spiderweb grimes my teeth. I force my eyes open so I can see that I'm not on a four-wheeler ripping through the woods, that I'm rocking slowly up a slope behind the snorting strength of two steaming, earth-smelling horses.

But Mr. Rosenberry has tensed. I watch his back straighten, then his head crane forward. His hands tighten on the reins, and the horses plod to a stop. "Damn kids," he mutters. He's looking down a side trail, a place where the weeds and brambles have been allowed to grow between timbering years. The thorny bushes have been flattened by what looks like an army of four-wheelers. Tread marks circle and swerve, gouging holes in the soft soil of the woods.

How could we have been so careless? I will him on, my eyes closed. My lips move, but I can't form a prayer. How close are we to her grave?

Mr. Rosenberry shifts and half stands.

"Daaad . . ." A wheedling voice comes from the back of the wagon. "Do you have to get so bent about a few tracks? Check it out later."

I glance at Lauren Rosenberry and send her silent thank-yous.

"Fine, but I'm coming back. These kids have no respect for property, and if I find signs of drinking or drugs, I'm calling the cops."

It's all I can do to keep my vomit inside as he flicks the reins over the horses' backs and we continue up the hill. I sit clenched and silent as the girls sing camp songs I've long forgotten. At the top, Lauren pulls out a basket, and her dad spreads a blanket. I eat nothing.

It isn't until we start down the opposite side of the hill that I untense. We wind along similar trails, meeting the farm road at the bottom. Soon we're at the barn.

"Aren't you the antsy one?" Maggie says when I long-stride it to her car.

I'm thinking of Shelly, of Angela, Victor, and Andy. What's Andy doing? Has he cracked, or did Victor visit him also? Maggie's words drag me back toward the norm, but there will never be a norm again. Still, I have to try to hold on to "normal" as long as I can. "What are you doing next weekend?" I blurt.

Playing shy, she bows her head slightly so she can look at me through a fence of lashes. "Nothing. Why?"

I swallow my fear that she'll laugh in my face and say, "Do you want to go out with me?"

"Sure," she says.

"Where do you want to go?"

"I'd like to see that new romantic comedy." She smiles.

I manage to grin back. "I could do with a laugh. How about Friday?"

The circling girls close in.

She nods and opens the car door. "Should I take you home?"

"Drop me at the bottom of Gremlin Hill," I say, not mentioning that I have to work off some of my tension or Mom will know something's up. Angela won't sleep, either, with my nervous energy bouncing around the room. She'll lie there, her eyes following my every move, the accusation there, always. Murderer. Twice a murderer after last night. I've tried to redeem myself, first with my oath to God, now with an oath to the devil—or the devil's helper, Victor.

I shudder, but Maggie says nothing. The other girls give me a look that says they can't believe she brought me, that I'm inept, a goon.

Maggie, though, drops a hand from the steering wheel and cups it on the seat between us. Just as casually, I allow mine to edge against hers. We aren't holding hands, yet a message I'm afraid to interpret drifts from her skin into mine. Another promise, but this time someone's promising *me* something, maybe even hope. But I don't deserve what Maggie's offering.

Still, I don't pull my hand back. I need this gift.

10

MICHAEL

"[If it] has little,
it will gain; . . ."

If Helen's parents accepted us for who we are, things would be easier, even now that we're separated. Then I wouldn't worry that they're sitting around the kitchen table bad-mouthing me, telling Helen that she should dump me since I ran out on her. Not that she'll believe them, but she might wonder what's up if I don't call soon.

From the day they first heard my name, Helen's parents never trusted me. The more they hear about me and my family, the more reasons they have to hate me. Even Richie's mom and all her miserable problems with my idiot dad are marks against me.

So is my career choice. They're afraid Helen will decide to embrace art, too, and they don't want that. She's good at drawing, when she works at it, but that doesn't mean she wants to do it for her whole life. Her parents should let her go for it if she wants, though, even if she fails. Moshie says many people try lots of things before they decide what they want to do.

The Mitchells don't like Helen hanging around Moshie,

either. He's the best influence as far as art and life go, but try convincing them of that. As far as they're concerned, he's a drug-abusing, drug-dealing creep who's leading their daughter astray.

Of course, their son-in-law's steroid use is fine. All it earned him were a massive neck, huge shoulders and arms, and a chest like a burn barrel. It's all turning to fat now, since he doesn't do more than play the occasional backyard game of football with his friends. His brain capacity stayed small, though. He hates me because I wouldn't "share" once during a test. Helen's parents also don't count their regular cocktail parties as drug events. But I do. I've seen what drinking too much can do.

But the main reason Helen's parents hate me isn't because I like Moshie and take Helen to his store. They hate me because I'm artistic. I went to her house for dinner once, and her dad implied that any guy who was artistic and not athletic was gay. Which doesn't exactly fit me, since I was dating his daughter, but logic isn't his strong suit.

Helen says he just opens his trap and lets fly the first thing that comes into his head. He once said, "Women shouldn't enter politics. They're too moody."

"Are you referring to PMS?" Helen said.

He shook his head. "Just stating the facts, and watch your tone. I'm your father."

His jaws were on overdrive during my senior-year art show, too. My favorite comment about the guest artist's piece: "The texture on that thingie is interesting, sort of like potholes filled with rubble." He said that in front of Mrs. Winthrop, our art teacher, who sponsored the show.

I'd entered several watercolor landscapes, but Mr. Mitchell

looked for the most abstract pieces and acted like they were mine. He stood in front of them and flapped his jaws about "nonrepresentative art," as if he knew what he was talking about. Helen had only let him come because she needed him to drive her.

He called Helen's pottery "planters without plants" and laughed. No one else had. Then he said, "Helen, what are your jugs supposed to hold?"

I couldn't believe he'd phrased it that way, but he didn't notice that he'd said something wrong.

"Hold?" Helen was almost as mad as a mother bear separated from her cubs.

"Yeah, what are they for? Do you make lemonade in them, or are they for storing grain?" Mr. Mitchell twirled a pot as though looking for a label.

"Grain. Right, Dad. We need to stash this year's harvest in the basement." She shook her head, gave him her you-dumb-ass-grown-up look, then said, "They're decorative."

"What's the market for them?"

"Market?" she hissed. "Art isn't about 'markets.'"

"Ah, art." He stuffed his hands in his pockets and rocked on the balls of his feet like a teacher about to lecture on the morals of the current undertwenty generation.

She didn't give him the chance. "Come on, Michael. Let's look at some of the other exhibits." Helen grabbed my arm and dragged me off. Mr. Mitchell's jaw swung loose on its well-oiled hinges. He probably didn't know how insulting he was. I had to keep him away from my paintings. He might scare off a potential buyer with his stupid comments.

But I shouldn't have worried about potential buyers. What he did was worse. Richie's grandparents, the Wagners, had braved coming to the show, despite Dad's orders to stay away. They weren't supposed to keep away from the art show specifically, just from anyplace they might bump into Richie. Dad has full custody of Richie; he doesn't share.

Helen and I were examining some freshman's attempt at sculpture when Mr. Mitchell began holding forth about my paintings to Richie's grandparents. They looked scared, like kids caught touching their dad's favorite gun.

Mrs. Wagner tried to derail Mr. Mitchell. "He's come a long way since Katherine had him. Look at the details." Mr. Wagner squeezed her arm.

I sauntered toward them, keeping an eye on the door. Nervousness crept over me like a spider looking for flesh to bite. *Dad won't come,* I told myself. *It's safe to say hi.*

But Mr. Mitchell didn't stop, despite the polite coolness of Mrs. Wagner. "Sure, he has the details right. But who wants to see them? I thought they were gentle landscapes from a distance, but they're really glorifications of trailer trash. Probably the kid's house. Those twisted, hay-bale–lined mobile homes, and the half-finished sprawl of that shack! Not a pretty picture. I wouldn't pay a plug nickel for it." He looked at Mrs. Wagner's shocked face, then asked, "Your grandkid?"

"No, no," both said before moving to another display.

Mr. Mitchell gazed at my stuff. "I never like being deceived," he muttered. "They make me feel peaceful—until I move in and see the squalor. Paintings should be of nice things." He'd turned toward the next exhibit as though he wanted to keep up with Richie's grandparents.

But Helen stood in his way, arms crossed. "What did you say to them? Why are they leaving?"

"Who?"

"That couple! The ones who were standing here."

"Why? Who were they?"

"People," she said, suddenly secretive. "Michael wanted to see them."

"Oh, Michael wanted to see them. Well, then I'm sorry I scared them off. I asked if they were related to him."

"You didn't! No wonder. Dad, don't you listen to anything I tell you?" She grabbed my arm, and we hurried to the door. But we were too late. I'd probably never hear what they thought of my pictures, and they'd never hear that I'd sold two of them or that Richie had gotten straight A's. They were gone.

But my father stood in the door, his tall, angular frame radiating anger. "Michael," he boomed as though he wanted to be sure every person in the tiny gallery noticed him.

Helen leaned close to her dad and hissed, "See, see?" in his ear.

"Did I see Kathy's folks leaving?" Dad said to me.

I wanted to shrivel into dust and float away.

Maybe it was selling my paintings, maybe it was Helen beside me, maybe it was the safety of a hundred people around me, but for once, I wasn't taking his crap. "Did you?" I said.

But Dad knew no one could protect me. "Liar," he said. "You're not allowed to see her family. She knows that, they know that, and you know that. You are my son, not hers." He spun on his heel and left without looking at my paintings.

I waited for his truck to roar past, then I headed for the door.

I shoved my hands in my pockets. My rage seemed strong enough to knock people over. *Like father, like son,* I thought.

Helen followed me, and Mrs. Winthrop asked Mr. Mitchell to make sure I was okay.

I guess Mr. Mitchell couldn't be bothered, because he never came by the gazebo where we sat. I didn't expect him, and Helen didn't want him. It was enough to be together.

If only her dad would lighten up and not judge me by my father, then maybe I wouldn't have to write notes to Helen's friends to let her know I'm all right. I could call her without scheduling a time.

Please give her the postcard, Shelly. Fast. How long can she listen to her dad run me into the ground before she starts to believe his lies? I couldn't take her doubts. I need her more than air, water, or food.

"Wait for me, Helen." I sigh. "Wait." Then I sleep.

11

JOSHUA

"... in my thoughts ..."

I don't hear anything besides the normal crap about Helen for two days.

"They did drugs and were probably busted or got so high they ran off."

"They fought with her parents, and she ran away."

"There's a serial killer on the loose," is one of the wilder rumors, and I act concerned for Angela. My fear is real, even if the rumor's not.

The newest rumor to circulate is, "He took her to New York City, and she's posing nude for artists." This doesn't even make sense. How could they have found an apartment or jobs so fast?

I've wondered out loud about their disappearance, too, mostly because I have no clue where Michael is—or what he remembers. Does he remember the party? Does he remember Victor giving him the drug? Is he in police protection? Maybe the drug didn't work. Maybe he followed our tracks and found her. Maybe we didn't leave those tracks behind, maybe the police did.

Without the Rosenberrys knowing? No. If the police searched their land, Mr. Rosenberry would know. Heck, he never let anyone on his property without permission. He'd posted more NO TRESPASSING signs than the whole county combined. What made us think of burying her there?

I didn't think of it. Victor or Andy did.

Neither acts fazed by the tension and rumors. They're going to classes, talking, and speculating like everyone else. Is that how I seem to them? Or do I look like I feel, like I'm going to explode?

Victor and Andy keep broadcasting their theory—that Michael and Helen ran off together—so loudly the police probably have heard. Maybe they even called the sheriff with that tip. It's not beyond Victor. He's cockier than ever, and the only sign that he's uptight is that his fuse is shorter. Yesterday, he knocked out a kid's tooth for bumping his books off the sink ledge in the bathroom. I was surprised, because Victor usually takes his revenge off school grounds.

Andy's dad bought another gun yesterday to replace the one missing from the cabin. Did Michael take it? We left it in the bedroom. Planted evidence, Victor had said. Or did Andy freak out and go back? Did he hide the gun? Or do the police have it?

After two days of thunderstorms outside the school and rumor blasts inside, I arrive to find Shelly in the center of a crowd. Her voice is hushed, but since no one else is talking, I hear her as soon as the door closes.

"It was from him."

"When did he send it?" pipes a girl who sounds like Angela. But Angela only haunts the school's corridors in plaques won and trophies given. Outside, a tree planted in her name shades the music room. I hate it. It's too much like a memorial, like she's dead.

Shelly says, "I don't know. It was in the mail yesterday. My parents made me call the police."

"Did they come over and search your house? Did you have to go to the station?"

"Don't be stupid." Shelly's not looking too good. The way her eyes turn, frightened and big like a horse's, doesn't help. She drills me with those wild eyes when she spots me. She has questions, and she thinks I have answers.

I head down the wrong hall, intending to double back to my locker, but then Maggie calls my name. I have to stop for her, so I turn, and sure enough, Shelly's next to her. Her coltish legs jiggle, and her eyes leak tears that she refuses to wipe away.

"What's going on, Josh? I thought they left together," Shelly says.

Oh my God, I think. *I don't have a story for this.*

She barrels over my silence. "It was romantic, you know, them eloping or something. Then I discover that his dad kicked him out, and now I get this postcard from him—Michael—for Helen. I showed it to the police, and they asked who was there when I left. You were there, right? You and Andy and who else?" She chews her lip.

Don't say it. "I think that's it," I say, but she talks over my disclaimer.

"Victor. He was there, wasn't he? You guys and Michael and Helen. What happened, Josh?"

I glance from Maggie's trusting eyes to Shelly's scared ones.

The lie comes easy. "I don't know. I fell asleep on the couch."

Heat rushes to my face as soon as I say the words. *Forgive me, Father, for I have sinned,* I think. What if Andy says something different? I'll have to call him and compare stories. I should call Father Paul, beg his forgiveness, have him take me to the police station. Why did I lie?

Shelly's shoulders collapse like a bird's wings broken in flight. "Then you don't know. I called the Underground Art Gallery," she says, which means she doesn't go there much. The regulars call it the Underground. "They didn't pick up. The message machine cut me off before I could ask about Helen and Michael. Where are they, Josh?"

I focus on Michael. "I don't know. He'll show up, don't you think?" I shrug. I won't have to confess about this since I don't know where he is.

The girls' eyes show that they know something's wrong. I bolt for class, wrong books and all, because I don't want to bump into anyone else. My words chase me through the halls to the second floor. "He'll show up." But what happens when he does? What does he remember?

I grimace. The teacher sees me and asks if I'm okay. I nod, although I want to puke. At home, when everyone's asleep, I run the water and barf and barf and barf. I see Helen's face and the dirt falling on her. Her hands stiffen, relax, then swell. Her body bloats like a road-killed deer, and her guts spill from her anus.

I raise my hand. "No, I'm not okay." I try to stifle a gag, but the teacher notices. "Could I lie down in the nurse's office?"

I run from the room, visions of maggots and the stench of a rotting body chasing me.

12

MICHAEL

"[If it] has much,
it will be confused. . . ."

I don't know what I was thinking, calling them. They hate my
guts. But I didn't expect them to send the hounds of hell after
me. Helen obviously wasn't home, but they wouldn't say where
she was. All they did was scream. Her dad took the phone from
her mom and said he'd kill me when he saw me again.

Makes me want to go home real soon.

What happened? Did Helen really take off with someone
from downstate? Maybe a girl, or a group of kids on the run?

Sometimes runaways blow through town on their way to whatever big city promises a future. They all find Moshie, and he
takes in every one. They live above his store, kind of like I'm
doing here.

Will Richie wind up like that? A runaway searching for his
mother and brother? I have to get him out of there. But how? I'd
have to go to court and prove what kind of a monster our father
is, and I can't afford that. Pounding fenders and stocking shelves
doesn't pay lawyer bills.

Not that I mind working. Mr. Lockwood says I'm doing great. I work in his original store, his favorite. He's here, too, most days. I live above the store in two rooms that haven't been turned into storage or office space. He used to live up here, but he has a nice place now. I haven't seen it, but I'm guessing from the clothes Mrs. Lockwood wears and the way she talks about stuff she's thinking of buying, like everything's there waiting to be chosen instead of being earned.

"It's my little retreat," Mr. Lockwood said when he showed the rooms to me. "For when the missus and I aren't getting along, or there's too much snow or ice to drive home."

I could read that as it's a place where he brings women, but I already know he'd never screw around on his wife, and he'd never kick his kids out. He didn't tell me all of his story, but he's made it clear that his dad was a bad one, if not in the same way as mine, then in another.

He reminds me of Moshie. Taking me in was a huge leap of faith for him. I work my butt off stocking shelves, taking out the trash, and ringing up customers so he doesn't regret picking me up.

But after my call to Helen's, I'm wondering if I can pull this off. My girlfriend's parents think I'm a waste product that should be eliminated. My dad threw me out because I want to be an artist, even though I say I want to be an architect or engineer. What have I done with my life since graduation? I planned on having my associate's degree this year, but I haven't even taken a college course. What the hell am I doing?

And now my girlfriend has run off, probably with some guy, or else she thinks I ran out on her.

No. Not Helen. She knows I'd never do something like that. I love her. She loves me. She wouldn't dump me.

Something's terribly wrong, even more screwed up than my dad could possibly make it. I just don't know what's up. I roll over and stare at the phone. There's no one to call. Not even Moshie. Not after the Mitchells' attack. I'll lay low and hope it all works out. It always has before.

13

JOSHUA

"... and in my words ..."

"Don't you know anything?" Andy berates me over the phone for being out of the loop.

"I came home sick yesterday, and Mom made me stay home today, too." Vomit, vomit everywhere. I'm lying on the couch until Dad comes home, trying not to infect Angela, who can't be moved from her bed. The doctor says it's temporary, but I've noticed she's not "there" more and more often. Her eyes are vacant pits. I watched Helen die. I'm afraid of what that vacancy means. My sister's leaving us, and I don't know who she is. How could God let her die? Is it because of Helen and how she died? Why did I help cover it up? What if what I did means I've forfeited Angela's life? But that can't be. I won't let it. Angela can't die.

My hand closes over the diary I've been studying, as if reading it will hold Angela here. I figured out the symbol for *e*, because it's the most common letter. The letter *i* was easy, too, because she started so many sentences with it. I had *f, o, t, r, s,* and *h* down, and was pretty sure of *n* and *a.* I'd know all about her soon, everything she thought and felt. Maybe then I could find the thing that would hold her here. There had to be something she loved more than life itself.

"Hey! Holy man! Are you in there? I said, they found her," Andy squawks.

The diary clatters to the floor. "Who? Angela?" I pick up the book.

"Helen, you idiot. Don't you ever think of anyone besides Angela?" He chokes, then goes on. "Helen. They found Helen." Hysteria makes him squeal, and he breaks off. Sobs catch and tear Andy like a claw in a nylon shirt.

"When? How?" I ask, but I know. I see Mr. Rosenberry looking over his shoulder at the ripped-up path. The sun's shining today. He'll have found the grave. He'll have called the police, eager to catch whoever fouled his land. "Holy Mother of God," I mutter over Andy's ranting explanation.

"Holy nothing. You have to come over to my mom's. We have to get our stories straight."

"I can't." Angela's lying on her left side. In an hour, I'll turn her onto her back. In three hours, if Mom isn't home from her rare day of shopping, I'll turn her onto her right side. She's on a rotisserie, and I'm the crank. "Come here?" He won't. He hates our house, the smell of shit and urine. He hasn't been inside more than once since Angela came home.

"Fine," he says, and the seriousness of what we've done rakes me. I shudder and gag as he adds, "I'll be there in half, tops."

"See you," I say like an idiot, like it matters how much we plot and scheme. God won't let us walk away unpunished. I've tried to beg for forgiveness. I go at night to my sanctuary in the woods, rain or no rain, and pray. My knees ache from kneeling. I've prostrated myself before the altar I built, away from prying eyes.

But I hear nothing. I've lost touch with Him, or He doesn't want anything to do with me.

"He always answers your prayers," Gram says. "Always. We, however, may not like His answer, or we may not be ready to hear it."

"How was Angela's living an answer to my prayer?" I'd said the day the doctors told us they thought Angela would remain comatose—a vegetable—forever.

"You asked for it. You wanted her alive, but you didn't know what that would mean."

"No, I didn't," I'd said. "But are you sure that was His doing?"

She'd slapped me. "That was my doing," she'd said. "I could control it. I knew my choices. You prayed for Angela's life, and you were given it. We are never given a Cross we can't bear. God's answer to you—to us—is that Angela is our Cross. It may hurt like my slap, but it's the only thing we have."

I'd agreed then, thought of my deal. "I'll dedicate my life to You if you spare Angela's life." I'd repeated it over and over as I sat in the hospital waiting room. My parents huddled opposite and stared at me as though I was the reason they were there. Maybe I was.

But I hadn't realized I'd been praying out loud until Dad said, "Shut up, Josh, just shut up. It isn't in our hands. It's up to the doctors. We can't change anything for the better or the worse. We can only wait."

Mom had clutched my hand, smiled a thin, wavering smile, then ducked her head into her own silent world of prayer.

So they knew about my vow.

How did burying Helen on a lonely hilltop fit with that vow? How did getting my story straight with Andy so that we weren't caught fit? Victor? Maggie? How did any of it fit? If only I could find a reason . . .

Someone pulls into the driveway. I groan. Just as I'm beginning to see a pattern in the web, the threads snap as the car stops with a splatter of gravel.

I look out the window. It's Andy. I hurry to my room and shove the diary between my mattress and box spring. Then I turn Angela so I won't have to while Andy's here.

Angela reaches up slowly as she's shifted onto her back. Her hand wafts through the air like she's stirring water. Maybe I owe her a way out of this world since I've trapped her in her body?

I freeze. My breath rasps harder than Angela's. Her legs are twisted, one under the other, which means her circulation is probably cut off. But I can't touch her again. I'm afraid of who I am, who I'm becoming. Maybe if I told the truth I'd stop changing. I'd get back on track, and Angela would get better.

But what about Helen? Nothing will ever make her better.

Andy's banging on the door. Angela waves a final time, her lips part, and she gurgles, "Go."

I run into the living room. She hasn't talked since the accident. Not one syllable. Was that a sound, or a word?

I jerk open the front door.

"Settle down," Andy says. He's calmer. "We aren't caught yet."

Why is it a "we" thing? I didn't shoot Helen, he did. I could turn him in, explain everything, and return to my old life. Was that where Angela wanted me to go? Or did she want me out of her sight? Does she somehow know what I did?

But Andy sinks onto our sofa, not commenting for once about knocking his ass on the wood frame sticking through the cheap upholstery. He grins, but his face is tense, troubled. "Victor told me to give you this." His hand's outstretched, loosely cupped.

I can't move.

He shakes his fist. "He ordered me to deliver it." He pauses, then adds, "Or else. Come on. It won't bite."

Or else what? Andy's face is blank, wiped clean by fear. He won't meet my eyes. I edge forward, knowing I look crazy. Andy opens his hand. A small, flattened gartner snake curls on his palm in a permanent S.

I step back.

Instead of looking at me, Andy studies the dried carcass, the flat black lifeless eyes, the swirl of the body like the sweep of a pen. "Victor says not to be a 'snake in the grass.' He says you'd get his point." Andy jumps away from me. Is he trying to separate himself from Victor's threat? "Sends me here with roadkill," he mutters. He glances in my direction. "Do you want it?"

I shake my head. I don't trust my voice. If Andy can't smell or see my fear, I'm not speaking it. Why won't he stand up against Victor? What did Victor say to make Andy so afraid of him?

He opens the door and throws the snake into the bushes. He rubs his hands together to shed any stray cells. He's back to business. His business, which is to make sure he's not caught. "What have you told people about Saturday night?"

Bile slimes my tongue, and I press my hands into my stomach to contain my nausea. I sit on a kitchen chair. "I told Shelly I fell asleep at the party."

Andy's head jerks up, suspicion in his eyes. Damn it! Why did I say her name? She's Maggie's friend, and I don't want her hurt. I don't want anyone hurt.

"Shelly?"

"Maybe it wasn't her. Some people were asking about Helen and the party. If she was there and when she left. I said I didn't know because I'd fallen asleep."

"Does your mom know when you came home?"

"No, but she knows I was home for Angela's turning at four. We talked then."

"How often does she turn Angela?"

Stupid, stupid, stupid. Andy's frightened beneath his smooth exterior. He's noting everyone who knows we weren't home when Helen died. Had Mom noticed I wasn't there at two? She hadn't said anything. "She turns her at midnight, then again at four, and then at eight."

He relaxes, but when he puts his arms behind his head, his pits are ringed with sweat. He sees me noticing and puts his arms down.

"Andy?" I try to sound nonthreatening. "Wouldn't it be better to tell? I mean, what if they figure it out anyway? It was an accident, and if we wait, it might look like we did it on purpose."

"Victor was right. You're too chicken to do this." His coldness scissors my lungs, making it hard to breathe.

"I'm not going to tell, Andy. Not without you guys. But—"

"Forget the buts!" Andy explodes. "I didn't mean to kill her, and I'm not going to jail for an accident. I'd get manslaughter, for sure, but you helped put her in that hole, and I'll make sure you go to jail if I do. Is that clear?"

"As a picture."

"Good. This is what we're saying."

I tell my mind to pay attention, that this is important, but my guts are quivering. I can't believe we're having this conversation. I tried to stop it.

DID YOU TRY HARD ENOUGH?

Shut up! I want to scream, both to Andy and the Voice. Up until now God's presence was kind, firm, supportive, generous. This voice is harsh, demanding, judgmental. It's asking me to do what's right, yes, but if I tell, I risk Angela and Mom. Victor would kill them for fun. Even Andy has said he'd kill me. Is that what God wants?

I close my eyes and focus on Andy's droning voice. No emotion stains his story. No regret. No sign that he's tormented with vomit or voices. Why am I? I did nothing wrong.

ARE YOU SURE? the Voice demands.

I reject it, forcing myself to listen to Andy.

"Everyone left the party," Andy recites, "including Helen and Michael. We went to bed. You're lucky that you said you fell asleep. It fits our story. Helen and Michael returned. Victor heard them and let them in. They took his room, and he slept on the recliner in mine. You crashed in the small bedroom, opposite Helen's and Michael's. Victor said Helen and Michael were pissed at each other over something, but he didn't ask what. He heard them fighting, but we didn't. The gun was in their room. It went off, but Victor's saying that Michael said they were fine, so he went back to sleep. We left when we woke up in the mid-dle of the night. I took you home, which is true. Victor drove himself. Stick with the time you actually made it home."

There are holes in his story, but I'm too tired, too sick to point them out. I nod, repeat the story when he asks, then get rid of him by saying Mom is due home any minute.

When I'm alone I think about those holes—the fact that Michael wouldn't have known where to find the four-wheelers' keys, how Andy and I were able to sleep through the shot—especially since I was just across the hall, that there was an exit wound on Helen's body. The bullet wouldn't be found in that bedroom, and there'd be no blood in that room. Victor still has our bloody clothes. Maybe he buried them. Maybe he washed them. Even after you clean up blood, it shows when special chemicals are applied. And what if Michael was seen somewhere else when he was supposed to be in the woods, disposing of the body? What if we were seen or dropped something at the grave?

My hands shake. My head spins. I stagger to the bathroom and throw up. I can't keep anything down. Mom's threatening to call the hospital. She thinks I'm dehydrated.

Maybe I am and I'm hallucinating, because when I go to my room, Angela's still waving slow gestures. She gurgles again. "Tell," she mumbles. "Tell."

But Angela can't talk.

I WORK IN MYSTERIOUS WAYS. LISTEN!

I drop to my knees, say a whole rosary, and wait. Not even the Voice responds to my despair. Nothing but silence, except for my weeping.

14

MICHAEL

"For these reasons, . . ."

I've been in Pittsburgh for two weeks.

I bought a new pad of paper and pencils with my first paycheck, and I paid Mr. Lockwood for the food he gave me. I didn't tell him about the art supplies. Habits of secrecy are hard to break.

I've called Richie a couple of times, but he wasn't home. Guess the jerk stuck him in some after-school program. I hope he didn't do what he did with me, tell him to stay home and not answer the phone no matter what. Too bad I didn't work out a signal system with Richie before I left, but I didn't. I can't call at night. Dad'll be there. I can't even leave a message. He broke the machine last month in a fit because I'd forgotten to tell him he had a message. Like he couldn't look.

I've thought of calling Shelly, but I haven't had the chance. I've been working evenings, and her folks don't let her take calls late. But I have to know what's up. I have to send a message to Helen—and Richie. Maybe I'll call a guy from the garage. He might pass something on to Richie, but he's so horny, I don't know if I want him contacting Helen. Instead, I write another postcard, address it to Shelly, and leave it on my desk.

I slide the sketch pad under my arm and circle the upstairs rooms, looking for a still life to draw, hoping that will force me to stop thinking of Helen and Richie. In Mr. Lockwood's office, I spot a careless arrangement of keys, books, a cup with coffee slopped over the rim, and a newspaper underneath. An envelope juts out from under the paper, but it doesn't fit in the section I've blocked off, so I ignore it. I flick on a desk lamp for lighting. I'm deep into sketching the cup in relation to the keys, trying to get their placement right against the blackness of the headline, when the letters come together to make words. Then a sentence. Then the headline sinks in.

I'm staring at it, afraid to move for fear that my moving will make it real, when Mr. Lockwood comes in. He flicks on the overhead fan and light. He jumps, seeing me there, frozen except for my wild hair moving in the fan's breeze. He comes closer, but still I don't move. Something is moving on me, though. Tears pour down my face, ruin my picture, let Mr. Lockwood know I'm alive.

I wish I were dead.

He sits opposite me and pulls the newspaper out of the mess, ruining the still life. I move at last, look at what I've drawn, but it's all splotchy.

"'Local Girl's Body Discovered,'" Mr. Lockwood reads. "'Farmer Finds Body in Shallow Grave.'" He pauses, then tips the paper toward me. "Michael, I've been wondering about this all night. It arrived yesterday with the mail from my camp." He pulls the big envelope toward him but doesn't look inside.

I nod at Helen's senior picture, so alive, yet so frozen. So recent, too. I haven't seen it. "Helen," I croak. "It's Helen."

"I recognized her from your description." We sit in silence. At last he stands, pulls the notepad from my hand, then takes the 2B pencil and slides it into the container in the right spot. He crouches in front of me. Those blue eyes I've come to trust, the same blue as my mom's eyes, are weighing me as though goodness or guilt is visible on my skin. "Do you want to read the article?" he asks.

"No!" I explode, then, "Yes!" I grab it and read. I reach *shot in the abdomen* and throw the paper across the room. I hurl my body after it. I'm hitting things—boxes, file cabinets, the desk, but not Mr. Lockwood. Even when he comes up behind me and grabs me in a hug a bear couldn't break. He hauls me backward, and we fall into the desk chair, me on top, him heaving exhausted breaths beneath. I'm not breathing.

"Let it out, son, but don't hurt yourself."

My hands throb. There's blood on both. I flex them. Not broken. But Helen is. She's gone, and I didn't even say goodbye. I don't know how to do what Mr. Lockwood says, "to let it out." I've been taught to lock it up. Still his arms steady me, let me relax enough so that I can cry again, and I do, bent double on the lap of a man I met two weeks ago. I'm still crying when the kid opens the store downstairs, the phone rings, and customers arrive. When I hear footsteps coming up the stairs, I jump away. Mr. Lockwood lets me go. I face a poster from some old drug company as Mr. Lockwood sends away the salesgirl, a cheeky eleventh grader who's been making eyes at me. "I don't want to be disturbed again," he says.

Her unspoken questions bombard me, but I don't turn. She'll tell everyone I'm being fired, that I've been caught stealing or something, but I don't care.

"Michael," Mr. Lockwood says.

I stiffen. Here it comes. The accusation, the throwing out, the hatred.

"Michael, you're in a lot of trouble." He hesitates. "The paper says they're looking for you. It doesn't say you're suspected of her murder." He has the grace to strangle on the word.

"I didn't do it."

"Okay, then you need to tell me what you did do. You need to tell me what happened. Otherwise I can't help you."

"Help me?" Why would he help me? What was I to him but a Knight? The hated son of an angry, frightening man.

"Michael, I know you didn't do this."

I turn. I have to see his face so I can tell if he's lying.

"If you did it, why would you hang around here, knowing that eventually I'd find out? Why would you tell me first thing about how wonderful she was and how you wanted to marry her? Why would you tell me who you really were and not make up some fake name? Why would you spend your money on drawing supplies and repay me for your food when you'd need money to run? No, Michael. You didn't do it, but you were there. Maybe you know who did?"

I've never been trusted before. Never. My teachers didn't trust me, except that art teacher, Mrs. Winthrop. But what's on Mr. Lockwood's face? The belief that I did nothing wrong despite evidence to the contrary? A sheet stained from my having sex with Helen, the hairs she and I had to have left behind, they were all evidence against me.

I groan and slide to the floor. If I tell him that, what will he think? He has two daughters. How would he feel about me, knowing Helen and I—

What? Loved each other?

I look again at him—hands clasped, head low, sitting in the chair where he'd kept me from hurting myself. Where had he come from? Could he possibly know what it felt like to be me? Was he what I could become?

Not if I don't get help.

I draw a shaky breath and say, "Helen and I dated for a long time."

His head comes up, and his hands loosen.

"I loved her, you know. I could never—" I choke.

"Take it slow. Tell the truth, but take it slow."

It takes most of the day to reach that night. Things said and done take on multiple meanings, shades of gray I never saw. When I tell him about the vague memory of an argument, not the actual argument, but the suggestion we had one from someone, he prods and prods, but the face behind the voice remains a blank. At last, he tells me to go to bed.

I stand, shaking, and reach out my hand. He clasps it, then pulls me close. "Trust me," he says. "It'll be okay."

I shake my head over and over. "No. Helen's gone. It will never be okay." I wobble from the room to collapse in bed. Later, when I wake, I go to read the article, to discover the when and how and where, since I can't put a why to it. But the paper's gone.

15

JOSHUA

"... in what I have done, ..."

Something's wrong. Even before I open the door to my house, Bach's tremendous notes crash through our double-wide. I stumble on the doorjamb. I'm able to keep from falling, but the notes set my muscles into spasms of fear. Mom only plays Bach when Dad's gone and Angela's bad off. She says it soothes her.

Gram, who took me to the doctor's, follows me inside, then freezes. Four beats later, she shoves past me, as though she can help.

I sink to the sofa. The news will come to me. I listen to the muttered voices and think of the doctor's response to my weight loss and near dehydration. "It must be a virus, but we'll draw some blood and do some tests."

I could've told him what's wrong. I keep seeing Helen dying, dead, decaying. But I have to keep from spewing what I know.

Mom's sobs almost drown Bach's *Jesu, Joy of Man's Desiring.* Gram sticks her head out of the bedroom door and says, "Make some tea. Strong. And find some liquor. She needs something to pull her together."

"What's going—"

"Do it!"

"Caffeinated or decaf?" I shout.

"Herbal," Gram says.

That means chamomile tea, which isn't good. Mom only drinks chamomile when she's really upset. I turn on the kettle and head for their bedroom. After the doctor forbid him to drink, Dad stashed the liquor in his file cabinet. A newspaper litters the sheets, and its headline catches my eye:

LOCAL GIRL'S BODY DISCOVERED. FARMER FINDS BODY IN SHALLOW GRAVE. My lips form the words. Then I'm saying, "Our Father, Who art in Heaven," but my heart registers nothing but absence. I stop praying. What's the point? I've broken my vow. God won't listen to me.

The shrill scream of the kettle forces me to my feet, and I grab the first bottle that comes to hand. I carry the tea and alcohol to Gram. Only then do I notice what Mom's so upset about, although the newspaper might have had something to do with it. Ever since Angela's accident, she's been abnormally upset about other people's problems and tragedies.

Angela's sleeping, but her breathing tube is shadowed with blood. The rings leading to her throat are clogged and caked with darkening brown, and only a small swatch of white tape holds the tube in her neck.

"What happened?" I hold out the bottle.

"It came off," Gram says, snapping open the seal on the

whiskey and pouring a shot bigger than Victor could handle into the tea. "Isn't that right, Rachel?"

"No, no, no. I told you, she pulled it—"

"And I said that's impossible. The doctor said she can't initiate independent actions. That's why we have to move her, exercise her. She can't do it herself."

But she does, although I don't say that. She moves a lot. They told us that her movements are unplanned, unwanted, jerks of a near-dead body. But what if we're wrong? What if she's in there, trapped? Held hostage by our care?

I can't think of that. I didn't make a deal with the devil.

Mom drinks the tea, holding the cup in both of her shaking hands. Blood's on Mom's fingernails and fingertips. What happened?

A bottle lies in Gram's lap. A little brown bottle with little white pills that send Mom on little trips to heaven. When she wakes, she won't remember.

Gram leads Mom to her room, so I sit on Angela's bed to clean her up. Her eyelids flicker but don't open. I reach for cotton balls and alcohol. I find a new breathing tube and take it from its package. I carefully swab around the tracheotomy, cleaning it of blood, germs, struggle. I loosen the old tube and quickly hook on the new one. I swab where it touches her skin. How had Mom put the catheter back in place alone? What had Angela done to pull it out? Didn't it hurt? Or can't she feel pain?

I stroke her cheek, so smooth except for the few pimples by her nose. She's sixteen years old, has acne, her period, and a developed chest, but not a brain cell working beyond the most primitive. The oxygen hisses. Gram's reading Psalms in the quiet, dim room across the hall. Mom will be almost asleep.

I lean forward and say, "What happened, Angela? What do you want?"

Angela's eyelids open. Her arms stir the air. She gurgles. "Onnnnnn," she moans, but she isn't there. Not really. Any more than Helen is here.

My eyes sting with tears I won't shed. This can't be happening. Angela can't slip away. I will keep her here. I will become a priest like I promised, and God will honor His promise.

But what did He promise? Do I really know? I made a vow, but did He? I close my eyes.

When I open them, Angela's arms swim through air laden with hope and fear. I catch her circling hands and tuck them under the covers, which I shove under the mattress. "Go to sleep, Angela."

I draw the curtain between our beds—as if she can understand what I'm doing—and open her diary. I have deciphered the first few entries. I'm looking for something that will hold Angela here, but it's boring stuff. I didn't think Angela, with her incredible talent, was so stereotypically into boys and clothes and looks. At least I hadn't thought she was, but then again, we never had the money for her to spend on that kind of stuff. Anything extra went to piano lessons or travel to her competitions.

Not much was left for stuff for me.

But that hadn't mattered. Andy used to invite me on his family's trips. So what if they went to places I wasn't interested in, like Michigan for fly-fishing. I did like the ski trip to Vale, which had made Angela jealous. I'd been smug about it, too. I'd built it into an epic adventure filled with snow bunnies in tight ski outfits and incredible runs. I left out that I'd discovered I was afraid of heights when I'd reached the top of the first big lift and had to force myself to ski down.

No, she never knew I was a chicken.

I slump onto my bed and listen to the respirator hissing as it pumps breath into her lungs. Does she want to live like this? Or does she want to move on to whatever is next? Is she saying, "Let me go"?

My head throbs. I close the diary; I won't find the answers there. I need guidance, but I have no one to ask. I bury my face into my pillow and draw my sheet over my head. If I never left this room again, if I became a hermit, then I would never have to worry about life and its problems.

Except Angela shares my room, and Helen has invaded my mind.

I cannot hide.

16

MICHAEL

*"The sage holds onto unity
and serves as the shepherd of all under heaven. . . ."*

Mr. Lockwood has brought me to a lawyer's office. I sit tense, shaking, silent, waiting for the lawyer to begin. He studies the newspapers, including a local one I haven't seen. It came out today. I don't try to read what it says. If there's a picture of Helen, I don't want to see it. I want to remember her as I saw her last, not as my damn nightmares keep showing her.

I haven't slept much. I spend the nights drawing, mostly hands and outstretched arms. It's like Helen is calling from the dead. If it weren't for the fact that I have to get Richie away from my idiot father before he's permanently damaged, I'd join her. No solution has occurred to me short of kidnapping him. I'd like to give him to his mother. However, she's determined to get custody the right way, but that's taking too long.

With all of this racing through my mind, it's no wonder I can't sleep. Mr. Lockwood has noticed and given me some over-the-counter stuff. He says if that doesn't work, he'll make a doctor's appointment for me. I told him I didn't want to sleep. I hated what I saw.

He sighed and gave me this big lecture about the stages of grief and what to expect, and that I needed to take care of myself, too. Helen would want me to do that.

I didn't say, "Bull. She'd want me with her." I just thought it.

The lawyer, in his suit that costs more than my dad's trailer house, looks at me, his eyes serious. "Son, I need you to tell me what happened that night."

I glance at Mr. Lockwood. He nods.

"Didn't Mr. Lockwood tell you?" I stall.

"Yes, but I want to hear it from you."

I've run through every moment over and over again, like a movie on an endless loop. I check faces against memories, trying to pick her murderer from classmates, friends, enemies, strangers. But there weren't any strangers there. That's the weird part. We all knew one another, if only to say hi when we passed on the street or at a game.

Or at parties where one of us turned into a killer.

I start there. "I didn't kill her, but I don't know who did. It doesn't make any sense, you know?"

He nods like he knows, but I'll bet he's never met a real-life murderer. At least not the kind I know. Where I live, it's the man who "accidentally" runs over his girlfriend in his pickup, or the father who kills his wife then commits suicide, leaving the baby in the high chair, or the hunter who shoots his buddy because he's been banging his wife. None of these murders involve money. The motives where I come from are pride and property, anger and hate. And by *property,* I mean women, because half the guys I know view them that way. Still.

But I'm not like that! I want to scream. How can I prove I didn't do anything, ever, to hurt Helen?

I can't. So instead, I tell about our last night, trying to not make it sound cheap, but knowing it does. I end with me waking and leaving the house. I haven't told anyone about her sock. I don't want to see it marked as an exhibit and held up in court. It's all I have of Helen.

Tap, tap, tap. The guy's banging his pencil on his notepad. I must not have come across as honest to him as I did to Mr. Lockwood.

"Have you had any contact with your family, friends, or her family since then?"

I shift. Mr. Lockwood doesn't know about this. "Yes," I say. "I sent a postcard to her friend asking her to forward it to Helen. Her father would never have given it to her. And I—" I hesitate.

"Yes?" The lawyer's almost drooling.

"I called her house and got her mother and father."

Mr. Lockwood whistles, but the lawyer's smiling. "Do you remember what you wrote and what you said?"

I nod and repeat it, pretty much word for word. It's not like I'm going to forget any of it anytime soon. "Did I make it worse?" I ask. Not because I'm afraid. I wouldn't mind dying, but I don't want Richie seeing me on death row. I don't want to watch him grow up through glass, always seeing in his eyes that he thinks I killed someone.

"I don't think so," the lawyer says. He pushes the eraser end of his pencil into his lip. "It proves you didn't know she was dead. Of course, since you passed out, the defense might argue that you killed her, then passed out and blocked out the crime."

"A drunk person could have killed a girl with a shotgun, but how could he have disposed of her body if he passed out?" Mr. Lockwood's hands are kneading his thigh muscles.

"Exactly."

"Have you heard more about the evidence?"

"They're being pretty closemouthed about it. Probably hoping that the murderer will reveal some detail that only the police and murderer know." He turns to me. "You haven't read the papers much, have you?"

"Only the first part of the first article."

"Keep it that way. The less you know about this, the better."

I want to scream that "this" is Helen and that she's dead, but no one but me has said her name in the last hour.

I must be frowning, because Mr. Lockwood puts his big hand on my shoulder and shakes it. "You don't want to read that stuff anyway. It's not how I'd want to remember her. Go wait in the reception area."

I stand, run a hand through my newly cropped hair, and look at the lawyer. "You think I did it." It's a question sort of, a test definitely. Even if he's the best lawyer in the world, I don't want the person defending me to think I'm guilty.

He isn't surprised. "It's going to be hard to believe this, Michael, but no, I don't think you did it. I'm not basing that on who you are, or what you told me. I'm basing it on evidence, pure and simple. So you can trust me."

If he'd said he believed me because Mr. Lockwood had asked

him to, I'd have walked—hell, I'd have run. Instead, I nod. "Okay. Then I'll do whatever you say except plea-bargain, because I didn't do anything wrong. I have one condition, though."

Mr. Lockwood's head jerks up, and the lawyer's lips flick a smile. He's more used to my type than Mr. Lockwood is, I guess. "What's that?" he asks.

"Find out how my brother's doing, and see if you can get him away from my dad."

He wasn't expecting this. I can see it in the way his eyes dart to Mr. Lockwood's, in the way that tiny smile vanishes. But Mr. Lockwood grins, and then the lawyer does, too. "I'll do what I can."

I sit in the waiting room and rub my bleary eyes. The receptionist's heels' clackety noise and bits of conversation drift to me.

"Told you he's a good kid—"

"What have you heard about the new tarp—"

"Several sets of footprints—"

"The kid's a wreck—"

"Father's pissed but had to let the police in—"

"Bullet hole—"

I can't sit still any longer. The receptionist is pulling law books off the shelves. "Tell them I'm outside, okay?" I say.

She's youngish, say twenty-nine or thirty, and she smiles. It's not even a suspicious smile. "Okay," she says, and returns to work. Does she know they expect me—Michael Knight—to be charged with Helen's murder?

I almost laugh as I walk out to the street. Me kill Helen? How crazy is that?

17

JOSHUA

". . . and in what I have failed to do; . . ."

The weekend slips by with me feeling like a high-wire performer. Andy's suggested a dozen things to do, from the movies, to hiking, to partying, but I turned him down, using my upset stomach as an excuse. Since I didn't go out with Maggie and the stomach virus has laid low a bunch of other kids, my constant vomiting looks real. No one, not even Victor, questions the validity of my illness.

Victor probably feels pumped up on this terror and uncertainty. He's a paintball fanatic, probably because he likes shooting people. Once, I went with him, Andy, and a bunch of other guys, which is how I found out he aims for the face, which is against the rules. When I complained, he shot me at close range in the ass. I was bruised all over. Andy said I was soft and didn't comment on the black eye and cheek I had for a week after Victor "killed" me. He said I didn't understand how to play the game. "You're not supposed to let anyone hit you. Even an idiot knows that. How'd you manage to be pegged that many times?"

"Because I thought you went to base after you were shot."

"No one does that. They take revenge on whoever they see from the opposite team. What a loser. No wonder Victor shot you in the ass."

Victor was pissed at me for telling on him then. What would he do if I told about Helen? Kill me.

The school's silent. The police have been to see her teachers and the principal more times than Andy can count. He's my informant, but I wish he'd stay away. He says they searched his dad's cabin but wouldn't let his dad inside while they did it. "Might have had something to do with the way he acted when they said they needed to search the place. He went ballistic." Andy gave me a sheepish grin. "He'd kill me, you know, if I'm caught. He's always harping on hunter safety and how it's only the idiots from downstate and the big cities who give hunting a bad name. He claims he never drinks when he handles a gun, which isn't true, but it's not like I can call him on it. I'd had maybe ten beers, Josh. If he finds out, I'm done for. I'll never see the light of day, and he'll never pay for my college."

I can't help thinking that Andy won't have to worry about college because if his dad finds out, then the cops will know. But Andy's not being logical. It's Sunday, and he's so bored he's come over to my house. His eyes drift, stopping most often on the place where Angela's piano used to be and on the short hall leading to Angela's and my room. We used to have two rooms, but in order to make the place handicapped accessible, we had to combine them into one big room. No way were the hospital bed, wheelchair, and respirator fitting in the tiny cell where she grew up.

Andy recalls me to the present by saying, "No one wants to do anything. They're crying and moaning about poor Helen."

"What did you think they'd do, Andy? Celebrate?"

He whacks me. Hard. I ignore it. He's looking for a fight, and I'm not giving it to him. After a moment, he sighs. "Yeah. Celebrate. I didn't expect that, but I did expect it all to blow over quicker than it has."

"The funeral's tomorrow," I say between clenched teeth. "Maybe it'll blow over after that." It's hard to keep the sarcasm from my voice. I can't believe he thinks it will just "blow over."

But the prospect of life returning to normal has Andy looking like a little boy who has been promised a new bike. "Hey, you're probably right." He's not thinking of me or Helen or even Victor. He's thinking of Andy. Which is what he does when he panics.

"'Course, the police will be at the funeral, watching for someone acting guilty or like they don't belong," I add. That's what they do on TV, which I've been watching a lot of when I'm home sick, mostly crime shows. It's weird how comforting it is, watching the police nab the right guy time after time. Mom keeps patting my head and telling me it'll be all right, that Sheriff Radner will find Helen's murderer.

Murderers, I want to say, *and you're touching one*. What would she do if she found out I'd been part of the cover-up? I see her as she was at the hospital after Dad had dragged Angela from the pond. Her shattered face, the slime of tears and snot, the guilt that she hadn't been there to prevent it or save her.

Ah, but I was, and she hadn't judged me then. Would she look at me with hate and horror now?

Andy nods. His head goes up and down like a fishing bobber on waves. "Maybe we shouldn't go to the funeral. Maybe we should stay away."

"That'd look odd, don't you think? The three people who saw her alive last don't show up for her funeral. We've known her since preschool, Andy. My mom's altered my dad's pants so that I'll look respectful. I have to go."

"They don't know we were the last to see her alive. Be careful what you say." His eyes glitter briefly, and his hands clench and unclench. Then he sags. We're alone. He doesn't have to act tough. "Do you think *he'll* come?"

Andy hasn't mentioned Michael before. I don't want to think about him. I shrug.

"Everyone says he did it. You know that? They think he has his dad's temper."

"But his dad has never actually hurt anyone," I say. Unlike Andy's dad, who's pounded a few losers in bars but has never been charged. He weasels out with his charm and money.

"He doesn't have to. He's the coldest prick I've ever seen. Do you think he ever touches Michael? I mean, you know—" Andy's red. "Hugs him? And his hands are always shaking like he can't control them. Shaking and moving toward you when he's pissed."

"You have experience with him?" I ask.

"Only that time I banged into his dud of a truck. He slammed the door so hard I thought it would fly out the other side. He yanked open my door and started to drag me from the car before he saw I was with a girl. Thank God. If it'd been another guy, he'd probably have pounded us into pulp. As it was, he'd stood there shaking and swearing and staring at us like he wanted to kill us. Then he spun around and jumped into his truck and drove off."

Andy never says, "Thank God." But he just did. I don't mention it, though. Instead, I say, "Poor Michael. My dad's messed up, but he doesn't do much more than shout at me."

I look out the window. Dad's throwing rocks into the pond again. After Angela nearly drowned, he'd wanted to get it filled in, but excavators and backhoes are too expensive, especially now. So he flung the big rocks into the water, figuring they would make it shallower. He'd hurt his back lugging a huge boulder down the slope and pushing it in. It didn't even go all the way in—it wallowed in the mud, and he couldn't move it. So it sits on the side of the water like a bench, while the water eats everything else he throws. He's down to pebbles now, but the pond's as deep as ever. I swam in it this summer. I don't tell him that, though.

Besides, I can't say as I blame him for checking out of life. He didn't ask for an extra-large serving of crap on his plate. I did. And I asked for it not knowing the penance I'd have to pay. So I never say much when Dad's not functioning. Praying doesn't work for him.

But it used to be the way I made it through my day. Have a test, pray for an A. Have to give a speech, pray the teacher falls asleep. That one worried me, since I'd pretty much sworn I'd give a speech to a full church every week for the rest of my life. People would be waiting to hear my divinely inspired words. I used to believe He'd see me through. Now, when I croak out an Our Father, I feel like an impostor. What right do I have to pray to God? But I can't stop. I keep hoping for guidance, for an answer, for relief.

"Should I pick you up for the funeral?" Andy says.

"Who else are you taking?" I ask, cautious.

"Munger."

"I'll stick with my first plans," I say.

He gives me an odd look. "You do that," he says quietly. "But we'll be there, watching." I see the dead snake again.

I hitch my pants over my hips. They keep sagging. "I'm not going to tell, Andy. I just don't feel like being ragged on by you guys. Besides, Maggie said I could ride with her."

He snorts. "You won't get anything from her. She's tighter than a nun."

My face heats. "It's not about getting something, Andy. I like her, and she likes me. That's all I want."

He sneers. "Oh yeah. Your oath. If you didn't have that oath, I'd say you were a faggot."

"Maybe I am," I say into his spite-filled face. "How would you tell? Would I have some mark or is there a physical body type, Andy? What is it? Huh?"

He backs off, surprised. "I was just—"

"Yeah, you were just. Leave it alone for once. Leave everything alone."

"Man, you gotta learn to take a joke."

I don't say anything. A joke. Isn't that how all this started? I turn to watch my father struggle against the endless flow of the spring-fed pond. I don't turn when Andy calls good-bye. I'm busy, saying a prayer for my dad, but he doesn't stop flinging stones at the pond. He only throws them harder, bending and grabbing fistfuls of grass, leaves, and dirt, then whipping them at the water.

The water hisses as they hit, swallows some, floats others, but remains impassive otherwise. *Secrets,* it says as another batch of earth hits it. *Secrets.*

18

MICHAEL

"He is not self-absorbed,
therefore he shines forth; . . ."

"We're biding our time," Mr. Lockwood says. He hands me a stack of DVDs and some snacks in a plastic bag. The TV and DVD player appeared shortly after our meeting with the lawyer. I've been relegated to backroom status, and now that I have entertainment, I'm supposed to stay here.

Biding our time. For what? My sentencing? Of course, no one's charged me with anything, but it's coming. It's like the scent of rain on a hot summer day, rising on a wind so faint I can't feel it, but it's there—tantalizing, earthy. The change in pressure is everywhere, and eventually, the clouds will move in. Whenever a siren screams past, I cringe. They're coming.

I take the movies. "Thanks." I've seen half of them, but he means well. I want to ask for canvas and paint, watercolors maybe, and some fresh flowers. I want to paint flowers. I'm sick to death of sketching the junk in his office and my room. I have to find something different, something beautiful to draw so I can keep these ghostly shapes at bay. Figures have attached themselves to the arms I've been drawing. Forms draped in flowing robes, indistinct, timeless, without identity. I don't think they're Helen anymore. They're a sign of how alone I am—and scared. Sometimes they're demons that frighten me into believing that I killed Helen. At other times, they're angels bent on saving me. But if that's so, why can't I see them well enough to draw them? Even my thinking that they're angels scares me. I need to hang on to reality, not slip into insanity, where these figures are leading.

I turn to Mr. Lockwood, take a big breath, and risk asking, "Can I take some stuff from the pharmacy at night?"

His shoulders square off. It's the first sign of suspicion I've seen. Too late I realize he thinks I mean drugs to help me through the nights. But I don't explain. I run my fingers over the only drawing pad I have. It's filling up. I've crammed the white spaces of the original drawings with sketches during my sleepless nights. Mr. Lockwood watches my fingers and has the sense not to say anything until he understands what I'm asking. "What do you want, Michael? Some vases and fruit? A nice cloth, some flowers? I can't offer you landscapes, unless you want me to bring some vacation books."

I nod. "Yeah, stuff like that. Maybe some paints and a new pad. I wish I could show you what I mean."

He sits in his office chair, booting up the computer. "Come here. If you show me what you want, I'll order it."

I stay where I am, looking for signs of the old bait-and-switch tactic Dad used, but there aren't any. He's honestly offering to buy me art supplies. Trembling, I sit next to him and show him what I need, all the while wishing I knew what was going on with

Richie. Mr. Lockwood hasn't told me anything about him since I demanded the lawyer help find him.

"I know it hasn't been long, but have you heard anything about Richie?"

Mr. Lockwood bookmarks the site where the art supplies are cheapest. He also clicks the box saying that he wants his info stored in an account. "There. You can order what you need." He faces me. His eyes are tired; his face drawn. He's invested so much time and energy in me. What is he getting in return? A demanding kid who's never satisfied. But he doesn't make me feel like that. Instead, he says, "I called his school. They wouldn't give me any information, but since he's a lawyer, Mr. Harding managed to find some."

I don't like the way he stops. As a matter of fact, it terrifies me. I want to shout, *And?* But I stay quiet. I have to play this role to the end, and if I lose my temper or show any impatience, I'm afraid it will cost me his support.

Finally he puts his hands on his thighs and sighs. "He's been withdrawn from the school. The trailer you thought was your father's, wasn't. He skipped town without paying the rent, and the police are looking for him. Apparently he'd been hunting illegally, and the property owner turned him in. Your father went over to the guy's house and beat him up. When he returned home, the police had been there, so he packed up and ran." He hesitates, then adds, "He took Richie."

The silence lengthens. At last I say, "That's a mark against me, isn't it? All my life, it's been 'like father, like son.' People will think I did the same damn thing. Well, I didn't. And where does he get off stealing Richie?" I jump up and circle the room. My hand throbs with the need to hit something, anything solid, so I can force this aching anger out of me. The s.o.b.! He's taken Richie. I think of Richie's mom, of the sneak visits I'd planned so his grandparents could see him occasionally, and once, so his mom could see him. It wasn't her fault she was so messed up. She'd married a creep. That was her crime. Her sentence was pain and humiliation and finally rehab. She was dry now. She deserved to have her son.

And what of my mother? Did she want me? Not that a nearly twenty-year-old guy can return to his mother, but I'd like to know if she ever wished she had taken me.

"She ran away and left you," the jerk I call my father had said. "She never wanted you. I caught her taking the Pill to keep from getting pregnant. I took care of that and her. She got pregnant, then left you. She hated kids. She hated you. You cried all the time. Croup or colic or both. I don't remember. I do remember her leaving, though. She went out the door and never looked back."

He must have thought I was an idiot, telling it that way. For starters, I was five when she left, not a baby. And she'd boxed up my toys and clothes and put them in her car. The only problem was that Dad came home while she was inside, grabbing her suitcases and me. He took everything from her car and put it in his truck. Then he'd come inside.

Even now I don't like to remember what happened next. I see my mother, stoop-shouldered and crying, going out the door with a single suitcase—all he'd let her take. She turned on the porch, and he hit her—hard—in the face, spitting hate at her. "Don't try to come back. You're not wanted!"

She fell backward.

I screamed and ran for the door. He grabbed my arms in a viselike grip. He dragged me to his bedroom and threw me in the closet. Then he'd latched the clasp that was supposed to keep me from his guns but worked equally well at locking me in with them. I heard him stomp from the room. Right before the thin strip of light vanished, he said, "She ain't coming back. Ever. If she does, I'll kill her, so don't even wish for it. You're mine."

I didn't hear her drive away. I never saw her again. She never came to fetch me, and she would have tried, just as Kathy's trying to get Richie. She wouldn't have left me with him forever.

Then again, we moved two days later to someplace high in the mountains. I don't know which ones. He only told me our street name. I used to worry about how I would find my way home if someone took me or I was lost like Mr. Rogers on TV said happened sometimes.

Then I stopped worrying and started hoping for a kidnapper. He or she never came.

"We'll find him," Mr. Lockwood is saying. "This time he broke the law before he ran, and the police are after him."

I sit down hard, replaying everything from the night my mom left. The angry voices, the slamming of his fist into her face, her plunging backward to lie at the bottom of the six steps leading to our house. How she didn't move when I ran toward her. I raise my head to Mr. Lockwood, who's staring at me openmouthed. "Michael," he says, his voice distant and shocked, "are you okay?"

I collapse against the wall of my closet prison again. Hear fumbling under the trailer where Dad kept his tools, feel the sliding tears, but don't voice my fear. I don't want him in my face, hitting me. But I want my mom. It's not until the darkness has passed and I've finally fallen asleep that he comes for me, all smiles and forgiveness. Until I asked for her.

"Don't ever say her name again," he'd said, his eyes so hard they hurt to look at. "You don't have a mother. You hear? No mother. She's gone. She left us. We don't need her anyway."

"Michael!"

Mr. Lockwood seems so far away. I flip through memories until I find her smiling blue eyes, then they're gone, and I'm looking into Mr. Lockwood's eyes as he shakes my shoulders.

"Michael! What is it? What's wrong?"

I focus on the blueness. It's not the same shade, but there's caring in them. I close my eyes against the blue and say, "My dad broke the law before, too. But nobody knows it. I think he killed my mom."

19

JOSHUA

". . . and I ask blessed Mary, . . ."

"I am the Way and the Truth and the Light. He who believes in Me shall never die." The verse flows around and around my mind as I ride with Maggie and her mother to Helen's funeral. Mom wanted me to stay home and rest since I'd thrown up again this morning. If I stay home, though, I'll think, and I don't want to think because then I'll try to make sense of Helen's death. So when Mom went with Angela in the van they send for doctor's appointments, I'd gotten ready.

But I didn't count on the words repeating like a fountain's murmur all the way here. "I am the Way and the Truth and the Light. He who believes in Me shall never die."

Does that mean Helen didn't believe in Him? What about Angela? She believed in God, and look what happened to her.

So many people are expected, they're setting chairs on the lawn. The pastor directs them, then hurries back to the doorway, to greet and soothe us. How does he hold on to his faith in times of trouble? How will he face Helen's family? A limousine and the hearse arrive. Guys from school wait on the sidewalk to carry the casket into the church.

Maggie's hair cascades before me, and I almost touch it, as though her beautiful hair is proof that God exists. But the casket looms into sight. How can Helen be inside that gleaming box? How can she be dead? How could Andy have shot her? He wouldn't hurt anyone. Never in a million years. None of this makes sense.

Maggie tugs my arm. "Josh, come on, or we won't find a seat. Are you okay?"

I nod and follow her. Despite Maggie's grounding touch, an irrational fear swamps me. *This is Angela's funeral.* My knees cave, and only the press of the swaying crowd keeps me from sinking. Maggie steers me into a pew. A small golden cross glistens behind the altar. The sight of it makes my fear recede. This is the Episcopal church, so it can't be Angela's funeral.

Yet.

I plunge my face into my hands like so many others in the church. What am I doing at this funeral? Me, who buried Helen, sheltered her killer. Shouldn't God smite me?

Helen's sister strides down the aisle as though she's taking the field in a soccer game, but her face is white, strained, streaked with tears. Her husband trails her. How can Andy look at them and not reveal his guilt? How can I remain silent? Are Andy and Victor even here? It'd be suspicious if they didn't come, but I haven't seen them. If they haven't come and the police are here, maybe I can turn myself in.

Mrs. Mitchell, leaning heavily on her husband's arm, sways down the aisle. The agony in her eyes knifes me. I'd expected her to be sedated, but she's not. Her gaze flails the crowd as she passes. What is she looking for? Helen's murderer? She looks past me, the good boy, the one who helped bury her daughter.

Then the casket slides forward. Eight young men, none of them Michael, balance Helen's shell on their shoulders. They don't stagger or trip. Will I have to carry Angela like that? Who will help me? Andy? The pallbearers bend their knees at a signal from the pasty-faced funeral director and lower the coffin to a wheeled table.

I am lost in a sea of faces. No one knows my secrets, but my guilt pushes into my throat. I want to announce my complicity and turn the mourners into a lynch mob to attack me. Not Andy, though. They can have me, even Victor, but not Andy. He didn't mean what he did.

The priest's words roll in their inexorable order. " 'For none of us liveth to himself, and no man dieth to himself. For if we live, we live unto the Lord, and if we die, we die unto the Lord. Whether we live, therefore, or die, we are the Lord's.' "

But where was the Lord when Angela nearly drowned? Where was He when Helen stepped into the path of a bullet? Did He mean for these things to happen? To ruin Angela's life, to end Helen's, to shatter Andy's? What are the lessons in that?

I stare at the ceiling fan, watching the blades' slow circuits and wishing they were a plane's propellers so I could escape. *What about me? Can I reconcile my faith in God with what has happened? What if I can't bear the Cross God gave me?* I lower my head and weep. No one will find my tears strange.

The stench of too many flowers in too small a space and the press of too many bodies against mine forces me to stop thinking. My stomach twists like a cat whose claws are tangled in a curtain. I struggle to keep from throwing up. There is no Communion, and for that I rejoice. The taste of God would have turned me inside out, because I am not worthy. I need to confess and do penance before I can take Communion again, but if I do that, Victor would come after me. If I was sure he'd kill only me, I'd do it. But Victor might kill Angela or Mom or Gram first. While some might think it merciful for Angela to die, she doesn't deserve to be murdered.

"There are snacks and drinks in the reception hall," Maggie's mom says when it's over. "Do you want to stay? They have people available if you want to talk."

Talk? Do they expect us to tell who we think killed Helen? To confess? Panic pitches bile into my mouth. I search for an exit, although running would be like admitting guilt. Around me, kids shuffle pass. Their faces are smudged and blurred with tears. Then I understand. Grief counselors, the kind they bring in after school shootings and big car accidents, not police investigators, wait for us.

I tremble. If someone really listens to me, I'll break. I'm drifting toward the only visible door, which is at the rear, when Maggie takes charge. "No, Mom. Let's go home."

All the way to her house, I concentrate on two things, not throwing up and the vast emptiness my doubts have carved. Once I could almost touch God through my faith, but now I'm empty. Maybe I should talk to Father Paul.

If Maggie notices that I lose my precarious hold on my stomach's contents the minute I reach her bathroom, she says nothing. When I reappear, she's sitting on the sofa, soft music strumming the air and my nerves. It takes me three seconds to recognize Bach's *Brandenburg Concertos*. At least it's not his *Mass in B Minor*, which would have catapulted me out of there.

"Wasn't your sister a pianist?" Maggie's mom asks as she comes out of the kitchen with a tray full of Girl Scout cookies and some orange juice.

Both look nasty, but I take a glass and hold its coolness against my wrist while I decide how to answer. With the truth, I guess. "Yes. She won every competition she ever entered." *Don't ask it,* I beg, but she does.

"Will she ever play again?"

Maggie groans and nudges her mom, who's offering her the tray. Orange juice slops over the remaining glass. "She's completely paralyzed," Maggie hisses, trying not to let me hear, but I do.

Maggie's mom turns red, mumbles an apology and something about more cookies, and flees.

And we're alone.

"Sorry," Maggie says.

A couch cushion separates us.

"It's okay." My finger traces the piping on my cushion. "I'm used to it. Most people haven't seen Angela since the accident, so they don't know how much it hurt her."

"That's putting it mildly. It must be hard on you and your family."

I search her face for hidden meanings but find only acceptance and understanding. "Where's your dad?" I ask to change the subject.

"At work. He didn't know Helen, but Mom was her Brownie

leader. She's still festering because I quit my first year of Juniors. I'm in the church youth group, but it's not the same." She holds up a Thin Mint. "She buys cases of them. Since I'm an only child, she has no hope of molding a daughter into her shadow, so she runs the council and gets her cookie fix that way."

"Do you regret giving it up? I mean, you sound like you were forced into it."

"We're all forced into something, aren't we?" She gazes at me, and I'm floating on flecks of green and bars of brown, the hazel of her irises. "What did you give up?"

"Angela," I say without thinking. I bite my lip hard. I taste blood. I haven't lost Angela yet. She's still alive. God could still heal her.

She hesitates as though not knowing what to say. "I'm sorry," she says finally. "I shouldn't have asked that."

I shift on my green velvet seat. "I miss her music," I blurt to let Maggie know she didn't say anything wrong.

"Does anyone else in your family play the piano?"

"No. I wasn't any good, and Mom gave up playing when Angela—" I let it hang, draw a shaky breath, then go on, "She couldn't stand it anymore. She'd taught Angela when she first started learning, but she's quit teaching, playing, even listening. Except for Bach." I stare at the stereo. Maggie colors, then jumps up to change the CD. "Oh, no, don't. Mom says there's something inherently soothing to Bach." I leave out that she only plays it when nothing else will work on Angela. I also don't mention how it haunts me.

Maggie sits closer—in the middle of the two cushions. I ease my weight left and almost touch her with my shoulder. She sighs, and I do, too, as the music shifts from adagio to allegro. "Does it work?" she asks, draping a hand next to mine.

I touch her hand with my pinkie, a chant forming in my brain. The heat from her hand is almost visible. Like vapor tendrils touching mine, it strokes and entices. "What?" I ask, my voice not quite normal.

"Angela. Does it soothe her?"

A draft wafts the heat away. I shiver, straighten, withdraw my hand. She follows my example, a little patch of red growing on her cheeks. "Nothing really works, but it soothes my mom, and then she thinks Angela feels better. Maybe Mom's lack of tension makes Angela relax, not the music." Images flash through my brain: a trach tube laced with red, Angela being checked for damage. "Bach was Angela's favorite composer. She wanted to learn harpsichord when she went to college."

Lilacs. That's what Maggie smells like. Or maybe freesia. Mom has some freesia hand lotion with the same sweet scent. I inch onto my cushion, but the scent follows me.

"Who do you think did it?"

I stir uneasily. "It was an accident," I say, my voice insistent. Angela didn't know how to swim, but she went into the pond on occasion. She wasn't supposed to drown. She wasn't trying to kill herself.

"*Helen*, Josh. Who killed Helen? I can't stop thinking about it, worrying that it was some lunatic who will strike again. None of us is safe." Her eyes shimmer with unshed tears.

I take her hand and hold it, thinking of that lunatic, or rather of one of them. The one who sits next to her, chanting a vow that doesn't matter.

Her nails are perfect crescent moons at the tips of her long slender fingers. Piano hands. And her skin is soft and fleshy with strength and life. So unlike Angela's, who has thin, long skeleton fingers that twitch and emit heat but are not strong and alive. Helen's hands are cold with embalming fluid, clasped forever over a rose in her coffin. I don't know if they're long- or short-fingered or if the funeral home scrubbed the dirt from under her nails. I just know they're dead, maybe brushed with makeup to give them the appearance of life. They will never hold another person's hand as I'm holding Maggie's.

I inch closer again, touch Maggie's hair for the first time on purpose, bury my nose in its sweetness, let the silken strands glide over my face.

Even still, all I can smell is dirt. When we kiss, I feel like Dracula kissing a newly risen bride.

20

MICHAEL

"He is not self-revealing,
therefore he is distinguished; . . ."

"It would help if we knew where this occurred, so we can trace it. Do you know your mother's name?" Mr. Harding asks.

"Miriam," I say. Dad screamed it thousands of times; he never said it gently.

"No last name?"

"Only ours. Knight."

"If your father had a history of violence, and apparently he did, then maybe he's responsible for Helen's death, too." Mr. Harding leans closer to me. "Did he ever say anything disapproving about her?"

"He thought she was too good for me," I say. "Does that count? Said her parents would never let her marry me." But I don't think he'd kill Helen for that. Not for any reason, for that matter. He had nothing to gain by it.

Mr. Harding leans back, a trace of smugness seeping into his face. "Do you know what he did the night of Helen's murder?"

I cringe at the word *murder*, but he doesn't apologize. Maybe he figures I'll get used to it. "No idea. He usually went drinking on the weekends, but not with friends. He doesn't have any friends." Sort of like me and Richie. He never let us do anything. I had to sneak to do everything. Now I can understand why he controlled me so much. I had a secret he didn't want told. But Richie? Maybe he was afraid Kathy would steal him. I wish she had. "Maybe we should warn Kathy and her folks," I say.

"We have," Mr. Lockwood says.

"Did she ask about me?" I'm too pitiful, looking for love from them when they've lost Richie. Why hadn't I taken him with me?

He shakes his head. "No, Michael. She may not have known you were missing. She might have assumed you were with them." His explanation rings hollow.

"Yeah," I say. "You still can't tell me anything about the investigation?" The urge to find Helen's murderer, to trap him somewhere and kill him like the evil monster he is, has been growing in me. I fantasize about finding him first, disemboweling him, strangling him, slitting his throat. It's always a *he*, although I have no face or age to give her murderer. He has a voice—it's the voice that lied and said that Helen had run off with another guy. It had to have been him that killed her. Why else would he have cooked up that story?

Like he's reading my mind, Mr. Harding says, "It's better if you know as little as possible."

I stifle my questions, block my rage. "You are not your father," Helen had always said. But would she want her death to go unavenged? Don't I have to make sure that whoever did this is brought to justice?

Moshie knew the hollowness of "justice." He told stories

about how abiding by the letter of the law usually let criminals go free and punished the innocent. He'd never given me a pat answer. I'd love to talk to him now, but Mr. Harding and Mr. Lockwood said I shouldn't call anyone back home. So I swallow it all until I'm bloated with hate, worry, and fear.

The overwhelming fear that I will never see Helen again. I want to believe that she's there, on the other side, waiting for me. But what if that's a myth, some pacifying story told to keep us in line? No, I have to believe there's something, even if the Hindus have it right and we're reincarnated when this life is over. But then, won't she be sent to a new life without me?

"We'll keep looking for your father. You can be sure of that. It's pretty damn suspicious that he left right after Helen's death. The police will find him."

Dad'll never let himself be found. Besides, he isn't Helen's murderer.

I want to die, to go to Helen. To be nothing or something with her. That's what I want.

I close my eyes. I can't die, because I have to find Richie. Blackness, the color of earth and dank places, is all I see and feel. Maybe I look awful, because Mr. Lockwood says, "That's enough for today."

Mr. Harding agrees, and I'm free of the searing questions to return with Mr. Lockwood to his pharmacy, which is starting to feel like home. He installed a corkboard strip on the bedroom walls so I can hang my drawings. He bought me a new lamp and a drawing table. The bed has matching sheets and blankets now. Even his wife's in the act. She sent over a bunch of meals frozen in individual packages so I won't starve. Which isn't likely. I've put on five pounds since I don't do anything but sit and draw. Oh, and think.

She also sent me a journal with a note stuck inside that I don't think Mr. Lockwood knew about. It said,

Write down your memories of her now, while they're fresh,
so you don't lose those, too. Harvey says you loved her a lot.
It must be hard on you. Whatever you need, ask.

> Best,
> Judith

It was nice of her, but I can't write about Helen.

I can't draw her, either. I try and try. Sheets of failed drawings are stuffed under my bed. Already I can't quite see her, can't imagine the tilt of her head or the slenderness or length of her neck. I can smell her in odd moments as I restock shelves or when a woman passes in the store. It's like the products she used to bathe and perfume her body are haunting me. I escape to my room and make popcorn to drive the scents away. They still come, however, in my dreams, in the shower, at the microwave.

So I'm trying to forget by reading whatever I can find, by watching the DVDs Mr. Lockwood brings, and by writing long diatribes against my father and Helen's murderer in the journal. A clean page means I need to foul it.

And I draw my mother—as I remember her before, never as I saw her last. Rows of blue eyes stare at me when I turn on the light. Dark hair curls around cheekbones made prominent by her haunted eyes. I don't know if that's how she looked or if I'm taking my features and sticking them on a female face. I dream of her. When I wake, I fumble for a pencil.

Funny, but I don't dream of Helen. Part of me doesn't believe she's dead. Mr. Lockwood gave me her obituary, and I pasted it in the journal. It's sounds like it's describing someone else: *Helen Mitchell, age 17, died suddenly. She is survived by a mother and father, a sister, and a niece, as well as her paternal grandparents. She was preceded in death by her maternal grandparents.*

I take the *Post-Gazette* to bed. The old edition, because I'm saving my money so I can repay Mr. Lockwood. I read every obituary, trying to imagine the things left out of accountings of loved ones' lives. How many people who deserve to be mentioned are left out? How many of the dead hated the sisters, brothers, fathers who survived them? How many loved someone passionately but were despised in return? How many people died in their sleep? How many died in pain? How many killed themselves? How many were murdered? How many are at peace?

I've clipped dozens of these abbreviated lives, looking for a pattern, a way to total up the worth of a life in two hundred words or less. If I had to write Helen's obituary, I wouldn't have mentioned her family at all. I'd have said she was a flower God gave the earth that had been picked too soon. I wouldn't have hidden her cause of death in the word *suddenly.* I would have said, *Murdered, damn it!* I would have used two words to say, *It's unfair,* and another four to scream, *I want her back!*

But I didn't write her obituary. I was the one left out of the accounting.

21

JOSHUA

—

". . . ever virgin, . . ."

"I've missed our meetings. I tend to get caught up with my daily duties and not take time for meditation," Father Paul says. He grips his wooden cane and shuffles toward the rear of the house. He's in pain. Normally I'd pray for him, but not today.

"I've been busy, too," I say. The lie slips out so easily. I close the door behind me but have to reopen it to free my coat.

Father Paul examines me as I pull my arm from my sleeve, which turns inside out as I struggle. "You're thin, Josh. Have you been ill?"

"No." His face is so earnest, so worried beneath its shock of gray blond hair, that I immediately say, "Yes. The stomach flu. I'm still weak."

He nods and sits in what's supposed to be a breakfast room but is really a library crossed with a greenhouse. Orchids bloom in numerous pots. A huge hibiscus hogs a corner; its pink purple flowers lay like smudges on piles of theology books.

Like a punished child in time-out, I fall onto the small,

wooden bench beneath a shelf of African violets. I've had so many wonderful conversations in this room since Angela's accident. I don't like bringing my lies here.

But I must lie. Even though I want comfort and advice about my loss of faith, I can't tell Father Paul about Helen. I wouldn't receive any peace from confessing anyway. I'd only feel fear and guilt for worrying Father Paul.

I also can't talk about Angela since he thinks that I've come to terms with her accident. The trouble is, no one knows what really happened.

I slump. If I sat straight, I'd have to look Father Paul in the eye, and he'd see the lies on my face. I whisper into Father Paul's waiting silence, "I've been having doubts about God and my calling."

"That's not uncommon, Josh. You're too hard on yourself." Amusement lightens his voice. "You're almost too young to be certain of this decision. You have years before you take your vows. If you pray, God will help you to be certain of your decision then, even if you're not sure today." He says this kind of stuff so often, it must be a standard Catholic response. Plus, he usually tells me to enjoy the gifts God has given me.

But what if everything God's given me is awful?

Father Paul looks to see if his usual tactic has had any effect. I nod, but his words ring false. I have to be hard on myself. I can't let Helen rot unavenged in her grave. I know the answer, and if it weren't for Andy and Victor, I'd act on it. But do I have the right to endanger my family?

No. I can't tell Father Paul. I crumple so that my head almost touches my knees.

Father Paul's voice aches with tiredness. He needs more support than houseplants can give him. "Would you like something to drink? Some soda? How about something to eat?" He hands me a plate of cookies, but I give it back without taking any. "Probably a good choice. Mrs. Fisher made them, and she's not as gifted in the kitchen as she is in her will to serve." He thumps a sugar cookie on the table, then drops it among the others. "I'll have to put these down the disposal."

Is he avoiding my questions? Why else would he be going on about cookies?

But he's not avoiding me. I'm avoiding him. How is he supposed to answer doubts I can't say?

He tries again to soothe me. "Josh, no one said being a priest would be simple. It's not easy to be a person of faith. Life tests us. We've talked about that. How my arthritis, coming on when I was so young and leaving me crippled, nearly made me quit praying. Your sister's accident is another example. If life were easier for those who preach His word, we would never understand those we minister to and the world in which they live. So we love and lose and hurt."

A person of faith. Is that me? If so, why am I so torn? What if I only promised to be a priest to save Angela? Is that duty or faith? Can it be both? What does God want? "Have you ever felt that God withdrew from you?"

"Well—"

"Because that's how I feel. Like He doesn't care about me or anyone else. Like we're down here fumbling around in the dark, and He's up there with tons of flashlights, but He won't throw any to us." I grip my elbows to stop my hands from shaking.

Father Paul leans back and gazes out the window for a long time before he answers. "Two of my best friends died when we were in seventh grade. They'd been riding double on a bike. My mother wouldn't let me go too. If I had, we might have ridden three bikes. Or maybe I'd have slung my legs over the back of Kevin's bike. I don't know. Maybe my mother had a premonition. But they were killed that afternoon crossing the road between our neighborhoods. They'd done it dozens of times, alone and together. They'd done it with me. We always checked for cars. Always. To this day, I don't know why they didn't look that afternoon." He stops, and his mind flies to a place I can't follow.

But his face stays here, and on it, I see my pain echoed. Something stirs in my mind. Father Paul is still questioning why this happened. So questioning is okay.

After a while, he says, "I told you when Angela nearly drowned that my true test was my arthritis, but I lied. I am tested to this day by the loss of those two friends. The senselessness of it. My parents' inability to tell me why it happened didn't help. I prayed like they told me to. I prayed for their souls, but mostly I prayed to know why."

If Father Paul could find God through such a tangle of doubt, could I? "Did God answer?" I lean forward eagerly, certain that at last, Helen's senseless death will be explained.

A brittle, almost bitter laugh breaks from his throat. "No, Josh. He didn't. Sometimes there is no *why*. Sometimes life just *is*. That's a hard lesson to accept, when it comes into our lives, and it always arrives. We can't know why God lets things happen the way they do. We can only trust that they are for the good of all." He sinks his elbows to his knees and his chin to his hands. "For instance, if I hadn't spent so much time in seventh grade grilling God for answers, I wouldn't have been on speaking terms with Him when my arthritis hit. I might have turned that trial into a hate fest and blamed God and medicine and everyone in between. I might have blamed my parents for giving me the gene that predisposes me to arthritis. But I didn't. I already had a path beaten to God's door of questions and faith." He stops, and he straightens his back. His face smooths, and his eyes clear. He seems to glow, but that's probably me wishing for a miracle, something to put my mind at ease.

I nod, but he hasn't answered anything. He's only stirred the water so I can't see the bottom. "So I have to accept—" I say, but I'm thinking it's not so simple. Bad things can and should be avoided. I could've prevented Helen's death, Angela's accident, all of it, even if at the time of those things, I didn't know it. Couldn't God prevent them then? Or wouldn't He?

"Yes, you have to accept that bad things happen to people, even to beautiful young women like Helen."

My head cracks against the wall it pops up so fast. "How did—"

"You should have guessed I'd know what triggered this crisis. How many tragedies happen in a town of three thousand people?" His voice is gruff.

He thinks I'm wondering why Helen had to die, not how I'm responsible for the suffering of her family because I don't have the guts to tell what happened. I can't face him. I pull my hair over my eyes. Father Paul's waiting for my response with a slight smile at the corners of his mouth and a knowing look. He must think I had liked Helen. How can I get out of this without lying more?

"Helen had a boyfriend," I choke. "They were going to get married. I didn't *like* her. Not like that. But she grew up with me, you know." I stand. The heat in my face tells me that it rivals the hibiscus blooms' color. It's not Helen I've been thinking that way about. It's Maggie. Father Paul's too close to the truth. The little bubble of belief that had been growing on his words bursts inside me.

Father Paul pushes on the table, but by the time he's upright, I'm at the door. "Thanks," I shout. "I'll come next week at our regular time."

"Josh," he calls. "Come back! What did I say?"

I catch a glimpse of his stunned face as I slam the door.

I sprint for my bike. My eyes blur, and my nausea grows. I skitter to a halt at the bike stand. *Act calm. Running will only make people believe horrible things.* I long to go to Maggie, but she is part of the problem. Besides, I'd have to lie to her, too.

How can I claim faith in God when I can't tell anyone the truth? Even Him.

I close my eyes, fight down bile, then force myself to move with deliberation and calm.

But when the world comes into focus, Victor Munger leers out of his car window.

Without thinking, I spin away and race for the church. No one can hurt me there. I crash into the church's side entrance and rush for a pew. I've done nothing wrong. I crouch and attempt to pray. But the wall of doubt I've built is insurmountable. Still, the church's silence eases my mind.

The minutes tick by, and Victor doesn't come. I begin to hear the words I'm praying, try to find the strength to mean them. I pause to listen for a response. There is none, but for a moment, I feel peace. Or is it only that I'm safe from Victor? Either way, I relax.

Then the door opens, and I can't maintain my serenity. I crouch by the kneelers, convinced that it's Victor come to kill me.

It's Father Paul, though. He hums "Amazing Grace." He doesn't see me. He's gathering the Eucharist and wine for last rites. Who's dying? Not Angela! God, no!

But if it were Angela, I'd know. I'm not sure how, but I would. I close my eyes and wait. After a few minutes, Father leaves and I'm alone.

I don't rise from the floor. I think about faith and the path to peace I glimpsed. Will I ever walk on it? But I know that in order to do so, I have to come to terms with what I've done and what God did not, will not, do. I lie there, staring at the ceiling. Finally the pattern of beams crossing the vaulted ceiling puts me to sleep.

22

MICHAEL

"He is not self-assertive,
therefore he has merit; . . ."

Mr. Lockwood, Mr. Harding, and I are cruising down Route 6 toward where this mess all started. They say there's no danger in going back now. The danger lies in not telling my version of what happened. The paper had plastered my name and the headline LOCAL MAN IMPLICATED IN GIRL'S MURDER across the front page. I don't care much about it because the two people who matter, Helen and Richie, won't see it.

"We have to set them straight," Mr. Lockwood had muttered, shaking the paper shut again. He'd plopped it on Mr. Harding's desk. "They'll try him in the paper, and he'll never be free of it, even if a jury acquits him."

Mr. Harding had nodded. "I noticed, though, that the police only want him for questioning. Sheriff Radner's evidence is very weak and conflicting." He gave me a long cool look. He keeps doing that, as if when he isn't in the room with me, his doubts return.

Maybe they do. They creep into my mind every night and every day—whenever my brain's empty.

Even when that little slut slipped up to my room in her off-hours to proposition me with her draped legs and tight shirt. Her voice had been slow, casual, low. Her hands had touched me whenever possible, small strokes as she brushed past me or bent to retrieve a lost earring. But all I could think was that she was a trap. Something Mr. Lockwood and Mr. Harding had arranged to check on my true feelings for Helen. So I'd shown her the door, then crawled into my bed and cried. Helen had nothing to do with my refusal. It was all fear. My room stank with it.

I buried my head under my pillow and screamed, afraid of someone hearing, but more afraid of keeping my rage and fear locked up. I wanted to hit someone, the girl especially. I wanted to hurt myself for failing by allowing my body to feel, to react to her presence and sexuality.

Don't I love Helen? Am I over her already? Did I ever love her?

I choke, and Mr. Harding, sitting in the passenger seat, checks on me. "Tired?"

I shake my head, although I haven't slept in days. "No, sir. Just stiff. I haven't been outside in a long time." I shift my weight from my lower spine to my ass, which means I have to straighten up. Probably looks better anyway than sitting slouched in the backseat like a cocky jerk.

"Haven't missed much." Mr. Harding focuses again on his papers. Mr. Lockwood's driving so Mr. Harding can work. Mr. Harding had been pretty pissed when he found out his cell phone didn't work in the hills. "I have a conference call at three," he barked. So Mr. Lockwood pulled over so he could cancel it from a pay phone.

Rain pulls brown dirt from the hills and muddies the river that runs parallel to the road. Dirty cream froth swirls and sticks to rocks. The river threatens to leap its banks, but this is hill country. Water swamps the valleys after major storms, so houses sit on carved-out slabs of earth or on the tops of the hills where the river can't reach them. Only where the valleys widen are farms and houses built on the flat river basin.

We're on the last twisting course of road, which hugs the mountain on the left and plummets to the churning river on the right, when I look across the valley to a house I've been to dozens of times, usually to pick up Helen.

"Hey!" I cry.

"What?" Mr. Lockwood swerves, and his head swivels on deer alert.

I point at the blackened heap that's Shelly's home.

"A fire, I guess," Mr. Lockwood says.

"It's Helen's best friend's house. Shelly's house."

Mr. Harding looks up, his thin tongue running over his ChapStick–coated lips. "Shelly?" He shuffles some papers, "ahhhs" in agreement, then takes a last glance at the house. "We'll find out what happened at the station."

He's smiling, and I don't like it. That contented cat grin, shielding secrets and prejudices, makes me nervous. Is he trying to prove I did something or not? I twist in my seat, but Shelly's house is gone, hidden by a turn in the road. I can't even go there to recapture memories of Helen.

But Mr. Harding's right. We've no sooner walked into the

police station than the sheriff says that the latest incident has them thinking I had nothing to do with the crime. They do, however, want to talk with me.

I tell what I know. Again. I wait then, hands clasped and head down, for the sheriff to announce his next move. He surprises me, which maybe he meant to do. "We're going to take a ride out to the scene," he says, and my head pops up. His eyes don't leave my face. "There's something I have to check on, and we can finish our questions there."

My heart sticks, and my throat dries. I stand and edge toward the bathroom. My facial muscles won't move, but I can't tell if they've frozen in a guilty look or in shock. The sheriff watches me go, but he doesn't comment.

At the cabin, eyes follow me everywhere, but no one says anything. I had started to hope someone would tell me what they think happened, who was responsible for Helen's death, but they don't. Left alone, I note the place on the wall where the police have tagged a small hole. The sheriff sees me looking and pats my shoulder. "Bullet hole, son. Doesn't fit with their story, does it?"

"What story?"

Mr. Harding catches my eye, then says, "He hasn't read the papers or talked to anyone." He bends over his laptop on which he's tapping away, entering God-knows-what about Helen's death.

"Very smart." The sheriff gives Mr. Harding's back an appraising look. "He'll make mincemeat of the DA," he mutters to the officer who's been guarding the cabin, forgetting—or not—that his arm's draped around my shoulder.

I feel less like a suspect, more at ease.

Then he says, "So where did you go after you woke up? Did you touch anything? Take anything?"

The sock. But I won't give that up. It's all I have left of Helen. "The doors," I say, startled. "I peed, so the toilet. I checked the bed." I don't say for what. They already know about the stains. The bed had been stripped to the mattress.

Mr. Harding is beside me before the sheriff's finished bobbing his head twice in agreement. "We gave our statement," he says.

"Right," the sheriff says. "The boy looks awfully composed. He taking some medicine?"

The vial of little pills. Mr. Lockwood said they're for sleeping only. Until today, I've obeyed, but I couldn't face this cabin without something. I'd put one in my pocket and taken it when I thought the interrogation was done. I didn't want to screw that up. I'd stalled around then, pretending to take a crap in the john until the pill had a chance to work. By the time we'd driven here, I'd mellowed enough to stand when they'd opened the door and motioned for me to come inside.

"Only sleeping pills. He's troubled by nightmares," Mr. Lockwood says.

Mr. Harding frowns. Does that make me sound guilty? Even if some of my nightmares are about Richie and what Dad's doing to him?

I change the subject. "We passed Shelly's house on the way into town. What happened to it?"

Mr. Harding gives me a look that says I should have kept my mouth shut.

"Can't talk about that yet. Haven't nabbed the creep who did it." He sounds like he wants to burn the arsonist.

Which is when I remember that everybody in town is related in one way or another. Shelly's probably his cousin or niece. I nod and say, "Oh," in a little-boy voice.

I sit in a chair her murderer may have used and stare at the stairs and the door to the room where we'd slept that night. My head spins, and somewhere inside me, a scream rises, rises, rises. I want to kill whoever did this. I want to tear them into pieces smaller than snowflakes. But I can't say that. I can't even show it. I clamp my lips together. I clutch the chair arms until my knuckles feel like they're going to crack open. Someone, anyone, had better let me out of here before my scream breaks free and they realize how upset I really am.

Because I can see her, standing there, at the top of the stairs, as she'd done that night. Going to use the bathroom, then finding the empty bedroom with a lock. She'd stood there, framed by the warm pine paneling, and waved at me, an eager, happy wave. I'd grabbed a couple of bottles and headed up, feeling the wash of blood and urgency throbbing in my penis.

She'd been so beautiful.

23

JOSHUA

". . . all the angels and saints, . . ."

Andy finds me in church. "What are you doing?" he hisses as he sits beside me.

I stay in an upright kneel and ignore him. Did Victor tell him where I was? Did he send Andy to kill me? No, it was days ago, shortly after the funeral, that Victor saw me panic. What day is today? Not even the investigation into Helen's murder is concrete enough to help me differentiate one day from the next. Time flies by with only Angela's deterioration to mark it.

Angela can barely breathe anymore, yet I'm closer to her than ever. I've read whole sections of her journal, which makes me feel calmer. Almost like none of this has happened. I imagine the diary in my hands, see again the strange swirls and shapes she invented for an alphabet. I haven't read the last month's entries. I'm afraid that once I finish, Angela will vanish. My fear is stupid, but I cling to it still. I find no comfort anywhere else. Not even in the chapel in the woods. I came here to avoid reading Angela's journal, not to find God again. The path I'd glimpsed at Father Paul's house eludes me. Still, my legs kneel. My lips mutter. My hands clasp in supplication.

Andy smacks me. Not hard, but enough so that I look at him. He's blurry around the edges. His face twists. In disgust? Fear? Pain? His lips move, and I focus on them.

"You're drawing attention to yourself," he says. "You can't stay in church for hours and not start people talking."

But Andy doesn't understand. He's wrong. If I don't act prayerful, people will notice. Take this morning at breakfast. I couldn't eat a thing, but Mom's pleading eyes forced me to put food in my mouth. I'd thrown up twice in the night, but Dad must have taken a double dose of sleeping pills because he hadn't heard. As we ate, he'd turned to Mom and said, "He's coming around."

Mom had looked at me, her eyes critical. She was shaking the bag Angela's breakfast came in. I preferred to say that she was stirring it—a bit of a joke in an otherwise dismal life. "If you think so," she'd said.

"He slept late. I'm glad he forgot to go to church on All Saints' Day. He needs a break."

It was November 1? All Saints' Day? I'd dumped my cereal in the disposal and headed for the door.

"He's the one we should be spending time with. She should be in a home. She'd have better care there," Dad had said.

"Don't you insinuate that I'm not caring for her properly. If he needs more attention, what's stopping you from giving it?"

"What am I supposed to do, go to church and sit there with him?" Dad's voice had taken on a pleading tone, and I knew what he was feeling. Abandoned. Dumped. Betrayed by the one thing he thought would always make things right.

"If that's what he wants, yes!"

I was almost glad they were fighting. If Dad's noticing how messed up we all are, maybe he's coming out of his depression. "I have to catch my bus," I'd called when their argument paused. I'd slammed the door and raced for the stop, arriving fifteen minutes early, which gave me time to puke up the four bites I'd forced down. When the bus arrived at school, I'd hopped off and headed for the church. The driver, who I've known since kindergarten, yelled after me, "Hey, Josh, school's this way!"

"Dentist first," I'd shouted.

I didn't stop until I was kneeling in church. Mary's statue is directly before me. Since He's not listening, maybe She will. But She's not saying anything. I'd tried Joseph's statue, maybe because of Dad. But Joseph wasn't answering, either.

Andy gives me a sideways kick in the knee. I've been kneeling for two hours, so I topple over like an overloaded Christmas tree. I pick myself up and sit next to him. "You have to pull yourself together," he says.

"How are you doing it?" I ask, not bothering to keep my voice low. No one's here but us. "Doesn't it bother you? Don't you see her when you shut your eyes? I keep seeing her falling down the stairs or lying faceup in that hole. I can't stop the images, Andy. How do you shut them out?"

He's pale and swinging his head in more directions than necessary to make sure we're alone. "Shut up, you idiot! Man, I can't believe you. It was an accident. I didn't mean it. If I meant it, yeah, I'd be bugged by a bad conscience, but I didn't, so get over it."

"But it's worse that you didn't mean it. Then there was no reason for it. No plan, no purpose."

He grabs a fistful of my hair and pulls my head close. "Exactly, Josh. There was no plan. I didn't intend to do it. Should I pay for something I didn't mean to do? It's no worse than if my car skidded on ice and banged into hers, and she died. I wouldn't have meant that, and I'd have to live with it, but I wouldn't have to beat myself up over it, would I?"

His answer is no, but mine is yes. "But she didn't deserve it," I whine. "She didn't ask for it or do anything to provoke it. And you were drinking when you had your quote unquote 'car accident,' Andy. You were way beyond the legal limit, so in that sense, you're responsible. You were handling a loaded gun, pointing it at people, even if you didn't point it at her. You were messing with people's lives! We should have stopped you!"

"Listen to me, Josh Stedman." He tightens his grip. "I am not responsible for Helen's death any more than the manufacturer of that gun is for making it or my father is for buying it. It was an accident. I'm going to forget you said that I did something wrong only because we've been friends so long, but if you ever say something like that again, I'll beat the shit out of you."

I rub my head when he releases me.

"Church or no," he says. "I'll do it where I find you."

"Yeah, right. But, Andy?"

He's standing in the center aisle, and I've moved to the side aisle. "What, Josh?" He sounds tired, and in the filtered colors of the stained glass, dark halos gird his eyes, shadows haunt his cheeks.

"What about Michael? Victor's blaming Michael, and he didn't even ride in the car."

"Drop the damned metaphor, okay? What do you want me to do? Go against Victor? Turn myself in?"

I say nothing. But all around me I hear, *Yes, yes, yes*. A chorus of voices shouting an affirmative into the silence of my life. I spin, whirl, stare. My eyes bug, and my heart careens. I'm floating, flying, drifting on the unexpected comfort of the song.

Andy runs through the pew for me. His feet land awkwardly as he dodges the kneeler I left lowered, and his right hip bangs into the pew back with every other stride. He's not looking for the voices. He's looking at me, and his eyes are dark and worried as he bends over me—no longer flying, but encased in love, lying on the floor under the window of Judas Iscariot.

"Christ, you're bleeding," he mutters, but his voice is drowned by angels and saints. "I'll take you home. Can you walk?" He lifts me, and I smile. "You're a lunatic, you know that?" He puts his shoulder under my arm.

"Can't you hear them? Can't you hear them singing?" I whisper so I don't disturb the music.

"No, loser, I can't. You weigh nothing. Aren't you eating?" He's dragging me from the voices, toward the side door.

"'Go tell it on the mountain. Over the hills and everywhere.' That's what they're singing, Andy. Don't you hear them?" I want to say that's what Angela's been trying to say, that we have to tell, but he interrupts.

"Shut up!" He struggles with the door. "Shut the hell up!"

And the voices fall silent.

"Oh, Andy!" I touch my head and stare at my hand, which comes away bloodied. "Don't tell them to be quiet. They're beautiful."

Andy checks for people on the street, then half drags me to his car, shoves me inside, and roars off.

I wave at the church. "Good-bye!" I call. Then I laugh. If I can hear angels, I can hear Him. Angela will go to Him when she dies. He's real. She will not end in nothingness.

24

MICHAEL

"He does not praise himself,
therefore he is long-lasting; . . ."

They've left me at Mr. Lockwood's cabin, which I hadn't expected. I hadn't packed anything but a change of clothes, but the idea must have occurred to somebody beforehand because there's a duffel bag with my clothes sitting on a bed down the hall.

I roam the cabin, picking up stuff like a little outhouse with a sign saying how much money a visitor has to pay for a fart (more for a stinky one) and a dusty shadow box his wife probably relegated to the cabin years ago. Two of its holes are empty; the others have miniature china dogs. I check the cupboards and fridge. Juice, cereal, noodles, jars of sauce, and cans of soup. Nothing perishable except the bunch of bananas, gallon of milk, bread, and hot dogs we brought.

Mr. Lockwood had to turn on the hot water tank and the water pump. "We usually keep it shut off all winter," he'd said apologetically. "But it'll be all right to use it for now."

I'd nodded and said nothing. This is another test.

"I thought you might like some time to think." He'd put his hand on my shoulder. "Maybe go to your house. The landlord said some stuff had been left, and he wants to clean it out. I persuaded him to wait until after you had a chance to go through it." He'd said nothing about Mom or Richie. He's said little about either one ever since I announced that I thought Dad killed Mom. It's good to know he hasn't forgotten, though.

He left then, dropping an envelope on the table. It has fifty bucks in it and a letter giving me permission to stay at his cabin. He thinks of everything. He reminded me that "they'll catch the murderer," which I took as a warning not to go off in search of Helen's killer. I'd like to hunt him down, but I have no clue who he is. So I stare around the cabin, defeat sinking deep into my bones.

At least Mr. Lockwood's cabin doesn't resemble Andy's. It's low to the ground, with a single step between the "sunken" living room and the rest of the house. Big bay windows look down the valley, but it's far from the water. The cabin backs against the hill and probably gets next to no sun. I won't know for sure until tomorrow since it's dark and I'm all turned around.

I do know I'm not far from home—if I want to call it that. I'm also carless, so whatever I want to do, I'll either have to hitch or walk. It's stopped raining, which will help either way, but clouds still dim the night sky. It's cold, almost bitter with the damp. The cabin has a disused feeling. I don't bother with food. The pill's worn off, and I have a throbbing headache. I pee, turn up the heat, then crawl into the bed where my duffel bag rests.

I sleep like the dead, waking to the grating roar of lumber trucks in low gear. When the trucks pass, the silence comes. I'm alone. No Helen. No Richie. No art. My sketchbook and pencils are in my duffel bag, but it takes more than the right utensils to create. It takes inspiration and desire, and with Helen gone, I have neither, only a mass of wild, disoriented sketches. None is good. All I want to do is find Richie and her killer. If I knew how to do either, I would.

I'm useless. I can't avenge my girlfriend's death or save my brother from a life in hell.

But I can go "home" and look for clues as to where Dad took Richie. It probably won't change things, but it's something to do. I'm dressed, so I eat without tasting, then slip outside. The cabin faces south. Through the naked trees, the water glitters. If there are other houses nearby, they're hidden by the bulging shoulders of the mountain.

How far is Dad's trailer? Two miles? I go back inside, dump out my duffel bag, grab something to eat later, then set off cross-country. "Stay away from the roads," Mr. Lockwood had said. "There's plenty of angry people in town, and you don't want them finding you alone. Call for food if you need, and leave the money in an envelope on the door." He'd written a phone number on a piece of paper. "I've done it tons of times, then gone off to hunt or fish. Mr. Trumble sends a boy out with the stuff, and he makes change. If you run low, tell them to put it on my account. I'll call to let them know a friend's staying here."

But don't let anyone know you're here.

As though I'm the murderer. Damn, I wish I knew who I should hate. Who I should pulverize for tearing my world apart. It wasn't a great life, but it was mine, and while I had it, I had hope.

I hike up the switchback lumber trail behind the house to the peak and then set off on the flat path that runs along the ridge. If it were any month but November, I'd worry about four-wheelers or snowmobilers seeing me. The trail's boggy from last night's rain. No one will be driving it today. Besides, it's a weekday, and everyone's either working or at school.

After forty-five minutes of hard hiking downhill, I head back up the big hill, Gremlin, that's right before ours. I slip across the road where branches meet overhead and no fence inhibits my sprint for cover. Andy Grabbit used to live up here, and that Stedman kid. Andy lives with his mom now, but Josh is still here. They're in school, I remind myself, making my feet plod on. No need to stay out of sight.

Helen loved walking in the woods. We'd hike for hours in the summer, and she'd made me promise to buy cross-country skis this winter. I'm imagining her walking beside me when I come across a small path veering to the right. I pause, mostly because I'm winded. But the path's too wide for deer, and there're no hoofprints in the mud. I gaze down it, see an opening in the trees, and let my curiosity take over.

I step into a circle of light. Two piles of neat stones support a thick slab of slate under a huge maple, whose bare limbs form a canopy above. A cross hangs from a branch, which makes me think the stone is an altar. The path empties into an aisle. Close to the altar is a dirt mound with crossed logs pounded into the earth like a railing in front of it. It looks like a kneeler.

It's a freaky place. I almost expect tombstones or murmuring-monk ghosts. I glance over my shoulder, gauging where I am in relation to the civilized world. I glimpse the Stedmans' pond with relief. This must be Josh's private church. Knowing whose it is relaxes me. I run my hand over the slate and look closer at the cross, which is store-bought.

Crack!

I spin, expecting Josh, if anyone, and find Victor Munger standing on the path. "I thought you were Josh," he says. He doesn't move from the shadows.

"This his place?"

"Yeah. He comes here all the time. I wanted to talk to him."

But school's in session. They should both be there. I watch Victor, judge his size and position. He's a transplant from some big city on the East Coast. His four or five years' experience can't match my fifteen years of forest traipsing. I glance at his feet. Sneakers. He'll twist an ankle hiking these steep hills dotted with hummocks and cavities from fallen trees. I can outrun if not outfight him.

My neck hair bristles as he steps into the little clearing. He moves closer, his back slumped under the weight of a pack. I move around the altar stone.

Why am I worried about fighting? Is it only Mr. Lockwood's warning? Or is it the sound of his voice, his better-than-you tone? My entire body tenses. Now that he's spoken, I realize it was Victor who told me that Helen ran off with another guy.

"I thought you'd left town," he says. He doesn't smile or lighten his expression.

I glance at his eyes, and the hair on my arms rises. My being here wasn't part of whatever he's planned, but he's more than willing to take care of me, too. I suppress a shiver. I don't want him to think I'm weak.

"I came back," I say. He doesn't need to know more. His eyes are cold and narrow, like arrow slits in a castle wall.

"Wouldn't think you'd want to, given what's happened." He steps toward me as though to impress me with his bulk, but bulk doesn't necessarily mean strength or agility. *Run,* my brain screams. But I don't listen. Hate surges in me. If he was the one who told me Helen left, then he might be the one who killed her. Can I take him? Do I want to? Would that make losing Helen easier? Or would I throw away any chance of finding Richie?

I shrug. "I had a few things to tie up." I circle him.

He follows my progress like a too-fat cat watching a mouse trying to escape. He's confident he can take me. Why? He doesn't know me. Not really.

"Oh?" he says after a pause. "I'd have thought they'd tie you up."

I ignore his implication that I should be locked up for Helen's murder. What had he said that night exactly? What had he done? Why couldn't I remember more clearly? I'd drunk some, but I don't think I'd passed out. I step closer to the trail, not moving too far from him, because I don't want him to think I'm running away. His nose twitches as though he smells fear.

But I'm not afraid. I stop with that realization and face him. "Why aren't you in school?"

He grins a broad smile that has nothing funny in it. "Because I have business to take care of. Sort of like you and your loose ends. Although what Holy Roller Josh's shrine has to do with your business, I can't tell."

"What about you? What do you have to do with him?" As soon as I say it, I know it's a mistake.

He crosses the distance between us in long, catlike strides, his grace matched by his rage. "What I do is my business, Mike the Mechanic. So buzz off." Spit flies onto my face.

My hand moves up to wipe off the drops, slow and challenging, but that's what he wants. Me to start something. Instead, I grasp my duffel bag's handle. "Get out of my face," I say, but keep my voice out of challenge range. "I'm going to see my brother, and you're in my way."

He hesitates, then his grin returns. "Your brother's gone. Everyone knows that. But go see for yourself." He gloats at being the first to tell me the bad news.

I don't act surprised. "Yeah, so everyone says. But I know where he is." I saunter past, letting him chew on that. What with the slowness of his brain and the slipperiness of Dad, he'll be wondering for a solid ten minutes where in the county my dad's been hiding.

But I don't know where Dad is. When I reach the trailer, I don't find a note from Richie—not even in our hiding spot under the tongue of the trailer hitch. Richie left fast, and he didn't know where he was going. I search inside but find no clues about where they went or where my mother is.

I take what I can carry, mostly food, a few of Richie's school papers, and a drawing of his. Mr. Lockwood says the furniture and stuff belongs to the landlord, so I don't take any dishes or pots and pans, although they'd be handy. I can't keep depending on Mr. Lockwood. I do find one of my paintings stuffed behind the paneling, and I roll it up. I'll give it to Mr. Lockwood when this is over. Not that it's worth anything.

I close the door and stare at the muddy, rutted driveway and the bleak dirt yard. A toy truck huddles against a tree. I kick it. It rolls over, revealing a beat-up peanut can. I hesitate, then pick it up and pop the lid.

Michael,
Dad says we have to go. He put all my stuff in the truck. He
burned your stuff. He says we have to get away from Mom
and you. I miss you and love you, Michael. I'm scared. I
don't know where Mountaina is.
                                            Love, Richie

Montana. He's taken Richie to Montana, to a state so big, and so closed, it'll be impossible to find him. He'll go to ground there, hide out in a small, keep-to-yourself community like this one. But he made a mistake this time. He didn't take all of Richie's toys, and he left me behind.

"I'm coming, Richie," I say, forgetting that I can't go anywhere but Mr. Lockwood's little cabin. I stuff the note in my coat pocket and head off into the woods, turning away from the burned patch and the ugly trailer where I lived for fifteen years. I have to go someplace to think.

25

JOSHUA

". . . and you, my brothers and sisters, . . ."

"I saw her! She was going into the principal's office, and her parents were with her! She's going to tell, man. We're doomed."

Andy's voice shakes me out of my dreams. For a moment, the holy chorus of angels sings as it had in church, then nothing. A deeper voice rumbles, but I don't understand what it's saying.

"I don't know," Andy says. "He's been sleeping for quite a while. I gave him some of Mom's little helpers. They work pretty good, but not for long."

"He's going to break." It's Victor, and he's close. His bass voice vibrates in my ear like a sour note. "When he does, he better be out of my reach."

"He's fine," Andy says. He sounds strained, almost like Victor has him by the neck and is shaking him. I slit an eye to check, but Andy's looking out his window. It's dark beyond him, so I don't know what he sees.

"Well, if Shelly tells someone we were the last ones there, so what?" Victor says. "Michael was there, too, and we never told them we weren't."

"It's suspicious, that's all. She might know something about Helen and Michael that we don't, and she knows they weren't fighting."

Victor's head snaps up. "What did you say?"

"It's suspicious?"

"No, stupid. About the fighting. She knows they weren't fighting?"

"Yeah. She was Helen's best friend. They'll believe her, not us." Andy groans and sinks his head into his hands.

Suddenly Victor explodes, jumping Andy from behind and nearly knocking both of them through the window. "You idiot! You stupid mother—! Why did you have to haul out a gun at the party? Why didn't you make sure it wasn't loaded?"

Andy shoves Victor off, but Victor spins Andy around and punches him on the jaw. I stop pretending to be asleep as Andy jumps at Victor. "It was your idea to hide her body," he spits. "We should've called the police and explained it was an accident."

Victor sucker-punches Andy, who sinks to his knees, a slow moan flowing from his lips. "Shut up. What's done is done. We're in this together, so we might as well pull together. Right, Stedman?" He faces me, a greasy grin cracking his face.

I sit up and nod. "Together." I rub my neck.

"Besides," Victor goes on, "I took care of Shelly. When she gets home, she'll know better than to open her mouth again."

Andy staggers to his feet and grabs Victor's shirt. "What the hell did you do?"

"Gave her a little fiery retribution."

"What?"

"I threw a gas bomb on her porch. Don't worry. The neighbors called the fire department in time. No real damage."

"How do you know?" Andy almost shrieks.

"Because I watched."

His words shake the remaining fog from my brain. "You watched? That's, like, the cardinal sign of an arsonist. They watch the fires they set. My dad was a volunteer fireman. They always check who's driving past a fire."

"Anybody see you?" Andy asks.

"Do you think I'm stupid?" Victor jerks free of Andy's hands. "I watched from the hill behind her house. I parked on that abandoned road at the other end of her development. I never drove by her house."

Footprints, gas, a glass jar. What other evidence did he leave? And how did he know that no one was hurt? Had he watched them leave? I think about Mom and Angela. What if he did that to our house? We'd never save Angela.

But would that be so bad?

I'm shaking, and my stomach rolls over, plays dead. I just want to keep my stomach under control so that Victor doesn't see me puke.

"Get out." Andy stares at Victor like he's never seen anything more disgusting in his life.

"Excuse me?" Victor spins, puffs his chest. But surprise looms in his eyes, as it does in mine.

"You heard me. Get out of my house. You're certifiable. You're a nutcase. You're a loose wire, and I don't want anything to do with you."

"Listen to who's talking! You're a fricking murderer!"

Andy's on him in a second, fists flying. From nowhere, a blade flashes. I know the knife's not Andy's. Convinced Victor will kill Andy, I jump into the fight just as Andy throws a well-timed punch. Victor's head slams back, and I grab his knife arm with both hands. I twist and twist it until Victor's almost bent double with my clumsy technique, but finally he drops the knife. It thumps on the carpet. I don't let go of Victor, but I ease up enough so that he's able to stand upright. His head's cocked toward the pain in his arm, and his eyes are blurry from Andy's punch.

Andy crouches, picks up the knife, then wipes a hand across his cheek, where a fine line sheds red. He brings the knife to eye level, then rises slowly until his face is inches from Victor's. He slides the knife under Victor's chin. "You come back, and I'll kill you, too. Remember, Munger, I have nothing to lose. I'm a murderer." He flicks the knife along the soft skin at the base of Victor's chin. Another thin red line appears, but this one doesn't bleed as much as Andy's. "Get out of here, Victor," Andy says. "I'll keep the knife as a souvenir."

He half throws Victor down the steps. I follow them to be sure Victor doesn't try anything else. He screams obscenities and curses all the way to the door, but he goes. Fortunately, we're at Andy's dad's house. If we were at his mother's, the cops would've been here by now. At the door, Victor balks, so Andy shoves him out. Victor grabs a log from the woodpile like he's thinking of bashing us on the head, but I slam the door in his face, then lock it.

When I turn around, Andy's gone, so I hurry back upstairs.

Andy's in the bathroom, a towel pressed to his cheek.

"You made an ugly enemy there," I say.

"Yeah, well, what was I supposed to do? The guy's going to kill us."

"He might." I open the medicine cabinet, but Andy points at the toilet tank, where he put the bandages. I grab a couple.

"Seems like today's the day to put each other back together again, hey buddy?" Andy says. He dabs the towel against his cheek, then looks at the blood.

I stare at him, my hands in the sink under the hot water. He taps the base of his head, and I touch my own. A clump of my hair has been chopped off, and a bandage bulges there. I remember and nod. I rub soap into a wet washcloth and say, "Move your hand."

He does. His eyes don't leave mine, but I can't meet his. "What is it you saw?" he asks. "In the church? Your face—it opened into some kind of—of joy or something. What was it?"

I hesitate. He's always made fun of my religion, told me that I was crazy to believe that voodoo nonsense. Neither of his parents went to church. For him, there'd been nothing holy. But they'd always told him to do the right thing, at least up until the divorce. Then they hurt each other all the time, tearing at the ties that bound them, until finally they cut them, setting Andy adrift.

He looks so lost as I swab his face. I put hydrogen peroxide on his cut, but he doesn't flinch.

"Tell me," he says.

I feel his need to know. It's laced with fear.

But I'm afraid, too, so I shake my head. "I don't remember." I say it fast, keeping my eyes lowered so I can't see the disappointment in his. "Maybe it was lack of food or sleep that made me look weird." I want to cry, flee, hide. I've failed not only myself and God, but Andy.

He turns away, and I risk looking at him. He's crying. The salt tears fall into his wound. Still, he doesn't flinch.

I pat the skin dry around the two-inch long slice in his cheek, then put the bandage on, pulling the lips of the wound together like Mom taught me.

"I deserve that, I guess," he says in a soft and shaking voice. "I deserve a lot for what I did. But hey? I won't let that lunatic hurt you. All bets are off."

Why was Andy supporting me now? Did it have to do with my vision in the church?

I gaze at Andy, wondering how far he'll go to protect me. Will he kill Victor? *Will you protect Angela?* I want to ask. *What if Victor tries to take the only thing she has left—the right to die in peace?*

But I keep quiet. Only nod. When I walk home, I notice there's a fresh hole in the woods behind his house. If Andy had covered it with leaves, they blew away. I stare at it a long time before I connect his dad's stripped gun cabinet with the hole. For all his tough talk, Andy's scared. Scared enough to risk his dad's wrath by "losing" his guns.

I hurry home, my mind spinning from emptiness to fear to hope. After all, Andy called off the bet, and I heard angels.

26

MICHAEL

"Now,

Simply because he does not compete,

No one can compete with him. . . ."

I'm on the main road to what passes for a city around here—
nineteen thousand people, a Wal-Mart, and a mall. My thumb's
out, but no takers so far. I left everything but some clothes at Mr.
Lockwood's cabin so I'm not weighted down.

I didn't take Mr. Lockwood's money. I'm not running *away*.
I'm running *to*. How stupid I was not to have gone to Moshie's
sooner! He'd help me through hell if I asked him. Even if I had
killed Helen, which I didn't, he'd forgive me.

I think. Moshie liked Helen. He used to leave books for her
to read while he and I were talking art and she had nothing to do.
She'd devour books like *Silent Spring*, *The End of Nature*, and
Enough. They'd kindle passion in her eyes, and she'd try to dis-
cuss them with us. Moshie'd join in, but I couldn't. I don't read
much. If only I had painted her then, I'd have captured her at
her best.

But I didn't, because I thought I had forever—or until someone better than me stole her.

I could try to paint her now. My art things are stuffed in my bag. But I won't. It'll end like all my other attempts—in failure. I don't even plan on showing my latest drawings to Moshie. All those hands, reaching, grasping, praying, clawing. He'd think I'd flipped, especially if he saw the eyes lining the walls of Mr. Lockwood's apartment. No, I figured I'd draw at night at his apartment. If I had trouble sleeping at Mr. Lockwood's, I'll never sleep at Moshie's. Helen spent so much time there. There will be too many memories to see for me to close my eyes.

But I'll have to walk to Moshie's, which is almost forty miles, since no one's stopping and I can't join the endless flow of kids going shopping or to the movies like I used to. I hunch my shoulders against the world and the sun, which insist on pretending everything's wonderful. I set out at almost a trot, not bothering to thumb it when cars whiz past. Tires kick muddy water, and I'm coated and wet within minutes. Finally a cement trucker offers to take me to his plant. "It's not as far as you want," he says, "but you look like you need to put some miles behind you."

I nod and climb in. When we reach the plant, which is right before the New York–Pennsylvania border, I jump out and thank him. Then I head around the bend and over the bridge, where a buddy of the trucker pulls up and says he's going my way, do I want a lift?

So I arrive at Moshie's store about three o'clock, earlier than I figured, but late enough for Moshie to be there. The shop's dark. I try the door, but it doesn't give. He only locks it when he goes out of state. I climb the stairs to his apartment, already expecting what I find. The door's unlocked, but Moshie's gone.

His apartment, which is only a bedroom, kitchen, living room that's more library than anything else, and bathroom, feels abandoned.

I look for a note but find nothing. My message is still on his answering machine. Maybe he never listened to it.

I call the LPN who does the tattooing. When I say who I am, her voice edges toward panic. Before she can hang up, I ask, "Where's Moshie?"

"He sent me a letter saying he wasn't sure he was coming back. He enclosed a check to cover expenses and asked me to close the store."

I nod, as though she can see me. Then, before I can ask where he went or where his letter came from, she says, "Did you turn yourself in?"

"I've talked to the police." My face heats, and my tone becomes defensive. "I didn't do anything," I almost scream. Then I remember Mr. Lockwood's warning about angry people and not being caught alone. Was I stupid to come to Moshie's? Will she call the police and turn me in when I hang up?

"They let you go?" Puzzlement creeps into her voice.

"They only wanted to talk to me. I didn't do anything wrong. I want to know who killed Helen more than you do."

Maybe it's my urgency, but she relaxes. "Moshie said you didn't do it."

So I have that at least. Moshie believed in me even if he abandoned me.

But how do I know he abandoned me? What if he's looking for me? "Where is Moshie?" I ask again.

"I don't know. His letter didn't have a return address. When

I cashed his check, the teller said it was odd because the account had the exact amount for the check in it. No more."

"What about rent? Utilities?"

"He pays the utilities, and he owns the building."

"What about the kids? And the people who bought his art?"

"If they've called, I wouldn't know. I locked the store and haven't gone back. You know, it was pretty good of him to pay for my schooling. I already have another job at a nursing home. It's not tattooing, but it's okay. The people are nice, but boring."

I wait, but she doesn't ask why I'm at Moshie's apartment, so she must not have caller ID. "Well, thanks, but if you hear from him, can you tell him I'm looking for him? That I need him?" I want to cram those last words back into my mouth. I sound so pitiful, but Moshie always said to tell the truth.

And I do need him. I need the way he listened with his head tilted, like he was the dog I always wanted. No matter what I did, a dog would listen to me, forgive me, and love me. Unlike most of the people in my life—Helen, Richie, and Moshie excluded.

I pace Moshie's small apartment, pull books from shelves, swallow the memories of Helen reading, a book in one hand and a bowl of kettle corn balanced on her lap. She loved popcorn. I open a cupboard. It's full, as though he just went shopping. The fridge is full, too. An old milk jug with only a quarter gone stands beside a bag of wrinkled apples and spotted, mushy tomatoes. Leftovers huddle in plastic containers, their contents under bacterial attack. The food on the dishes in the dishwasher is so dried on it may never come off.

Moshie left suddenly. Why?

Was it Helen's death? Did he go to her funeral?

I play the messages again. Mine's the oldest. The others were recorded after Helen's body was found, with a week separating mine and the next. After that the messages flow unbroken to the present.

The living-room tables are stacked with books. A cup of almost evaporated coffee stands beside Moshie's favorite chair—the one where Helen read. I touch a book called *The Fabric of Reality.* Was Moshie reading it, or Helen? Or both?

My heart swells like the tongue of someone lost in a desert. I ache like I've been running for days. My breath comes shorter and shorter, and my eyes scorch with dry heat. No tears relieve me. I scan Moshie's shelves for a book that might offer me comfort or guidance about where Helen is now and whether I will ever be with her again. The closest I find is *The Way to Shambhala: A Search for the Mythical Kingdom Beyond the Himalayas.*

I sink into Moshie's chair. Bubbles of hysteria press against my throat. Helen in some mythical place in the Himalayas called Shambhala? How weird is that? She, however, would've liked the idea of going there when she died.

My laughter ends. Died. Helen is dead. I whip the book across the room. The pages flutter, flap, then bend as the book smashes into the shelves and flops to the floor.

Where's Moshie? He's supposed to be here. I need him. He's my rock, my salvation. I don't care what the people say about him—that he's a drug dealer and corrupts kids. They don't know what they're talking about. Moshie's the only one who took time from his busy life to listen and help us kids chase our dreams, even when they were as mundane as wanting to go home. He sent more runaways back to their parents than the police did.

For others, he found work so they would never have to go back. He admitted that sometimes kids shouldn't have to return.

But when I really need him, he runs away.

I storm into his bedroom. He didn't walk out in his underwear. He took something. A bathing suit for Cancún? A ski jacket for the Rockies? Nice clothes, not his tie-dye stuff, in case he went to an art show? Not that he traveled much. Most art dealers came to see his work in his studio out back.

In his bedroom a dusty box sits on his bed. Photo albums and newspapers litter the sheets. His dresser drawers are shut, and the closet looks full. A suitcase stands on the floor by the broken-heeled cowboy boots Moshie won't throw away. Since he continually sent kids home, he was always buying suitcases. Yet here stood the oldest one I'd ever seen. It was empty. Hadn't he taken anything with him?

I sag onto the bed. What does it matter what Moshie took or didn't take? He's gone. Maybe he thought I didn't trust him since I didn't turn to him right away, but I didn't know Helen was dead when I left. I curl into a ball, shoving aside the dusty, mildew-smelling newspaper clippings. The tears come.

But they don't last, because there's no room to let my rage loose. Too many people would hear the shrieks I can barely contain. I pick up the nearest clipping.

WOMAN, 22, CHARGED IN CHILD'S DEATH.

I read the article without registering much more than that she killed her daughter in a fit of rage over her wetting the bed. That and the quote attributed to the woman's mother: *"Lot of good them social services do, bothering folks in their own homes. She wouldn't have been so mad if social services hadn't taken her from me when she was young. It ain't my daughter's fault. It's the system's."*

I drop the clipping and grab another. It's dated a few months later, and it gives the details of the woman's trial, presided over by Saul Moshe Weinstein.

Could Moshe be Moshie?

There are several articles about the trial, and in one, the murdered girl's grandmother is carrying a sign and pointing at the camera. WHO TAUGHT MY CHILD TO MURDER? it read. WHO REALLY CAUSED JANEAN'S DEATH? is on a sign in another protester's hands. The next article describes the verdict being handed down. The article has a picture of the accused. She's blond, young, but with a hardness around her mouth.

I know that hardness. It comes from suffering at the hands of a "loved one" while God stays silent. It was around my mother's mouth; it surrounds mine. Will Richie's become weathered sandstone, too? I tried to shield him, but now he's alone with Dad. How will he survive? Will he become mean like Dad? Will he become a chickenshit like me? Or an alcoholic like his mother?

I whimper, then stomp my worries into a cranny of my heart. I glance at the woman's picture again, and for a second, it's Helen gazing at me. But no, there's no resemblance besides their golden hair. Helen's eyes weren't shadowed by hate and failure.

To rid myself of the image of Helen hurt and scared, I pick up the photo album. Who was Moshie? Was he this judge? The first page gives me an answer. Others give details.

LOCAL JUDGE VANISHES. NO FOUL PLAY INDICATED.

JUDGE'S DISAPPEARANCE ROCKS REPUBLICAN PARTY. NOMINATION TO STATE SUPREME COURT WITHDRAWN.

WILL JUDGE WEINSTEIN REAPPEAR?

JUDGE'S WIFE FILES FOR DIVORCE. WEINSTEIN DOESN'T APPEAR OR CONTEST.

A few more articles about the sale of a house, the graduation of a child appear, but the rest of the book is empty, like a promise broken.

"Moshie? I didn't know you, did I?" I say.

No one answers.

27

JOSHUA

". . . to pray for me to the Lord our God. . . ."

Shelly's at school despite the fire. I came despite the fact that I was caught puking in the locker room yesterday. The dozen terrorist/serial killer stories that were circulating were too much for my stomach. Victor's warning fire had fueled their spread and scope.

Shelly's house was pretty well trashed.

"The insurance guy said the smoke and water damage ruined more than the fire did. We were lucky no one was home, or we might have been overcome by smoke inhalation," Shelly's telling a group of kids, including Maggie.

"Do they know what caused it?"

I hover, trying to catch Maggie's eye one second, then hoping she doesn't see me the next.

"Arson," Shelly says, her voice low.

"Oh," say about twenty girls, who then break into the gaggle effect.

"Do you have enough clothes?"

"Where are you staying?"

"Do you need a ride to the game Friday?"

"How long until you can rebuild?"

Idiots! No one has asked if her family is okay. Did her dog escape in time?

Worrying about Shelly's family makes me forget about Maggie until she squeezes out of the crowd to take my hand.

"She'll be fine. They're all okay," she says, her voice like water on my scorching fear. "I'm glad everyone shut up about who did it, though. She's pretty upset about that. She doesn't have a clue why someone burned her house."

I look for Victor, but he's not around. God knows where he went. He's like a rogue policeman in one of those movies where they save the world by breaking the law. The problem is, the only the thing he's trying to save is his precious ass.

Like it matters. Like anything matters.

Maggie studies me. "Still feeling sick, aren't you? Did the doctor say anything?"

"Not much." I steer her away from the other kids. They don't need to know my problems. They think I'm weird enough as it is. They call me Saint Josh when they don't think I can hear. If they only knew. Demon Josh would be more like it. When we're out of earshot, I say, "I might have to go for some allergy tests, and Mom's talking about getting one of those mold crews in to test the house."

"It can't be that!" Maggie's too loud.

"No." I keep my voice level. I don't look at the kids who are heading for class. "I doubt it."

"So what—"

"It just is!"

She recoils at my anger like Angela used to when I babysat her years ago. I used to get so mad at her when she teased me about the scholarships she'd been offered. I'd hated that she was escaping so easily, and I'd be stuck in this dinky town. But I had no talent to pull me out of here.

I master my temper. I hold Maggie's arm, which is so warm and soft. "I don't want to talk about me. It upsets my stomach to think about it."

"Oh!" She colors. "Sorry."

"Don't worry about it." We're almost to class. I turn to Maggie. "Do you want to do something this weekend?"

"I'm going to the football game Friday, but we could go together. Or maybe we could go out Saturday?" Her eyes glow, and her face flushes.

I don't deserve her excitement, but I can't tell her that. "Sometimes my mom needs me to watch Angela. I'll check with her and let you know which night is better."

She smiles, and my cheeks pull up in a macabre imitation of a smile. By the startled withdrawal of her eyes, my attempt to look happy failed.

"I'll call you."

She nods and runs back the way we've come to reach her class on time.

I drift through the day, take a quiz with questions I don't recognize, only to find I've sat through a class that's not mine. The teacher has been watching me the whole time, taking notes, I suppose, to pass on to the principal and the police. What will they do? Haul in every distracted kid for questioning? But then, sitting through an entire wrong class isn't just distracted.

Titters float around me as I realize what I've done. I pick my books up and go to the teacher's desk. "Sorry." I lower my head. An untied shoelace curls like a snake on the floor. *Keep quiet. Don't give anything away. He'll kill you and Angela and Mom.* "I was daydreaming, I guess."

"Something upsetting you, Josh? Something out of the ordinary?"

Silence forms a wall behind me. They suspect me. I can't break free. I focus on the snakelike shoe lace and take the safest way out. "Angela. She's worse."

LIAR!

The wall of suspicion bends, then breaks in sighs and shrugged shoulders. *He's not a murderer*, they think. *He's a concerned brother.*

"Can I go home? My mom was up a lot last night with her, and I thought since I'm not doing any good here"—I wave behind me—"I could let her take a nap."

YOU ARE A LIAR!

I ignore this harsh, accusing God, but with each word He grows louder. I expect the teacher to hear, but she doesn't. Instead, she signs a note that I don't bother to take to the office. It's last period anyway. I bolt, glad I missed the bus that morning and had to ride my bike. I take a less direct route home, riding dirt roads to avoid being seen and to arrive closer to the woodland shrine I built. I want to try to recapture the angelic joy I'd heard in church. This judgmental God only torments me, makes me feel inadequate. I need to bathe in His soothing love, and the place that gave me that feeling most often before Helen's death is my sanctuary.

But when I reach the shrine, I find no peace. The slate slab I dragged from the mountain has been hammered and broken. The crucifix I strung up has been cut down, and when I find it, Jesus has been decapitated. The legs of the altar have been scattered and painted garish colors. Letters sprawl across the largest chunk of altar. DON'T TELL, they scream in vile green.

A wall of anger falls on me. YOU HAVE VIOLATED MY HOUSE. YOU HAVE DESTROYED MY CHURCH!

"No!" I shout. "I didn't do this."

THEN WHO DID?

I pick up a three-foot stone. The sharp edges dig into my hand, but I raise it above my head and fling it away. It shatters against a tree trunk, splintering the bark and leaving a gaping white gash. "I didn't do this. Not everything is my fault!"

BUT YOU WON'T ADMIT TO WHAT IS. YOU WON'T TELL THE TRUTH.

I'd always believed that no matter what I did, God's love would save me. But what I did is so despicable, I can't expect that anymore.

I sink against the dirt kneelers and shout at the circle of blue above the empty branches. "Where are You? Where were You? Don't You care? Don't I matter? Don't You want me anymore?"

When at last I stop venting and listen, I hear only the empty limbs grinding against one another. Branches moan in the wind.

It's nearly dark when I drop my head to the ground. I've failed to keep my end of the deal. It was me who broke the promise, not God. I helped hide a murdered girl's body. I brought Victor's revenge down on my sanctuary and my family.

Angela! Did Victor hurt her? I race along the path and burst into the house. Mom's at the kitchen sink. She turns. Words, questions fly from her mouth, but I don't stop. I bolt for my room and thrust open the door. Angela's there, her hands moving in slow motion above her head, the tube fastened to her neck.

I bang against the wall and laugh. Mom runs into the hall, her face lined with worry. I slide down the wallboard until my butt hits carpet, then drop my head into my hands. My laugh becomes broken hiccups and sobs. My eyes squeeze and squeeze, trying to pull tears from my wrung-dry eyes.

Mom lifts me, hushes me. Her hands can't silence me, but they get me off the floor and onto my bed. From somewhere a voice speaks, clear as an unclouded sunrise after a torrential rain. I still my frantic heaves to hear God's Word.

"Mountain. Go on mountain."

It's not God. It's Angela. Her left hand presses against the tube, and her lips move, pushing out words, notes. Angels join her in singing the old hymn.

But Mom bends over Angela, removes her hand from the tube, silences her.

"Stop it!" I shout and lunge to shove her away. "She's trying to tell me something!"

"Josh!" Mom screams. "Josh! Stop it!" She holds her hands over the tube, protecting it, but I claw at her. Angela gags. Mom lets go of the tube and spins around. She slaps my face. White-faced, shoulders heaving, eyes streaming, Mom stands with her arm raised.

I stumble back, feeling her slap like a brand.

"Stay away from her!" Mom warns. "Leave her alone!"

"I was just—she was trying to talk!"

"She was groaning. Nothing more. What's wrong with you, Josh? What's happened?" Her arm drops, and her eyes lose their icy glint. "She's your sister. Why would you try to hurt her?"

"I wasn't," I protest, but she shakes her head, turns to Angela, and assesses the damage. When she's satisfied there is none, she looks me in the eye.

"You can sleep on the couch. I can't trust you anymore. And you're going to the doctor's as soon as I can get you an appointment."

I shrink into myself. *Can't trust you anymore* tolls in my head. What have I done? I glance at Angela, but she's unmoving. I shuffle backward out the bedroom with Mom walking toward me, her arms full of bedding. She won't stop watching me now. I can't even ask her for the car to take Maggie out, so Friday— tomorrow—is a no-show, no-hope night.

Mom's eyes are on me, questioning, scared. I could tell her about the ruined altar, but then I'd have to tell her why someone did it, and I can't do that and protect her.

I curl up on the second-best couch. Will this push Dad into taking more pills? I tighten my hold on my knees until I'm squashed like a doll run over by a car.

The angels, locked in Angela's room, sing, chant, mock because I've broken my promise, ignored my vow. They should stay with her. She needs comfort where she lives: between life and death.

"Go tell it on the mountain. Over the hills and everywhere." I hum the song off-key.

Mom sits in the recliner, her eyes black pits in her too-white face. I wish she'd turn on a light so I could see her better, but maybe she's afraid of seeing me. At last she moves closer, reaches out. "I love you, Josh. You can trust me." Her voice cracks, and she sobs. "Do you want to tell me something?"

I compress myself smaller and smaller. She won't see me if I shrink to ant size. Could I shrink small enough so I could dance with the angels? On a blade of grass? On the edge of a snowflake? On the head of a pin?

Her hand strokes my back as I curl on myself.

Inside, in the emptiness, I'm dancing light as air.

28

MICHAEL

"The old saying about the bent being preserved
intact is indeed close to the mark!"

Night drags on Mr. Lockwood's hillside. I haven't gone inside
the cabin since I returned from Moshie's, and my hands are
freezing. I'm counting the cars heading west, away from town.
They comb the heavy air with their headlights, as though looking for an escape route. Is that the way Dad left with Richie? Is
this the road Helen's murderer took when he fled? When the
moon is almost above me, I reach a thousand—a thousand cars
leaving a town of three thousand people. Most of them pass
through without stopping. Just as well.

I stand, the stiffness in my legs nearly pitching me down the
hill. I hobble to the cabin and stagger inside. I search until I find
an atlas of the United States. I trace dirt roads, state roads, high-
ways, and interstates until I can estimate how long it takes to
drive to Montana. Forty to forty-five hours. That's too long for
Richie to behave in a car. Will Dad let him play along the way?
Or will he drive straight through, stopping to pee on the side of
the road or to grab some fast food? I peer at the yellow splotch

that's Montana. The map's not topographical, but I imagine the big skies and distant rugged mountains, flats and peaks, swollen rivers and frosted glaciers.

Dad can lose himself and Richie in the folds of those mountains. He probably won't settle near a school, and he won't teach Richie more than how to load a rifle and put the butt against his shoulder to steady the kick. But maybe, living there, that's all he'll need to know.

I sleep when the warmth reaches my toes and wake when they seem dead from lack of circulation. Dawn bleeds gray into the valley from behind the crest of the hill. It's almost seven, but I won't see the sun until eight.

I force myself to eat, shower, and change. Then there's nothing to do. No television, no books except the dictionary. I try to sketch, but I can't concentrate. So I stuff my pad and pencils in the bag and take out the tube Mr. Lockwood gave me for my paintings. I pull them out and sort them, debating which are fixable and which are not.

When I come to Helen's portrait, I lie down and touch her face. "Where are you, babe? Do you hurt? Do you miss me?"

Dampness seeps into the corners of my eyes, but I blame it on my position and sit up. I don't have time for emotions. I need to find her killer. To prove my suspicion that Victor is her murderer.

But how? Maybe I can find a clue at the Grabbits' cabin. I touch the painting of Helen again. I had tried to paint over the marker, but it didn't work. I might be able to have it matted so that most of the O will be hidden, or I could paste mementos over it to hide it. I snort. What mementos? Her sock? That's all I have. I don't even have a copy of her senior picture.

I almost sink to the floor. I'll never see Helen again. Maybe I'll never see Richie again. Moshie's gone, and it looks like I didn't even know him. Did I know Helen or Richie? What if Helen was only infatuated with me? What if Richie forgets me?

Well, I'll never forget either of them. The cabin boxes me in, makes my mind roll in endless circles. Like a caged bear, I stumble from room to room on the verge of exploding. I'm afraid of what else I'll lose if I leave the safety of Mr. Lockwood's cabin. Finally, I steel myself to face the Grabbits' cabin again, open the front door, and leave.

I walk down the drive and into the woods. How long will Mr. Lockwood let me stay here? Long enough for me to prove Victor is Helen's murderer? Would my confused memory of his voice be enough to peg it on him? I doubt it. I can't figure out why he killed her. He barely knew her.

My feet plod on and on, past trees stripped of leaves. My legs snag on hidden roots and fallen limbs covered by years of leaf clutter. I don't watch where I'm going, because Helen is everywhere, behind every tree, lying in every patch of watery November sunlight, throwing stray leaves in my face.

As I turn downhill, she dances next to a streambed. When I'm slogging uphill, she peeks from behind a boulder. I trail her for hours, wondering if this is insanity, God giving me hope, or the devil tempting me. I don't try to catch her, I just follow. My eyes feast on her face and hands. Her hair glints in the sun, and her feet and legs flash as she races ahead. It's a gift to see her again, even in this crazy way.

When the sun glides back toward the hills, I lose sight of her. I stand in emptiness shrieking her name. But she doesn't reappear.

Still, I don't cry. I'm too tired. My goal of finding the Grabbits' cabin takes over. I don't know where I am, and I can't do anything until I figure that out. I head toward the sound of cars, orient myself on the road, then head back into the woods. I'm not as far from the cabin as I feared.

I'm surprised when I come upon the tree farm. I didn't realize it was so close. I cut across the sheared spot where saplings grow in ordered lines, the pattern of rows and matching heights somehow wrong. I plunge into the woods on the other side of the field as the sun dips below the peak behind me.

If I head down the slope, along the dry runoff gully, then up and over the next peak, I'll be at the cabin where Helen died. I have to see it again. It draws me as though it can answer my questions, as though Victor will be there waiting for me to corner him.

Light shifts, changes. Shadows darken, deepen. Ahead, yellow and black ribbons flutter, the undergrowth lies mangled and shredded, and a pit gapes. Thoughts of revenge vanish. I know what happened here. I don't want to see it, but I can't turn away.

As though grief is a physical force, I stumble, cry out, and collapse. I bury my face in the dirt. Rocks gouge my flesh like bony fingers. I roll and sob. I fall into the hole. I lie where Helen lay dead while I worked and sent her postcards, thinking she was alive, missing her, wanting her. I claw at the grave's sides, trying to make the earth swallow me, but it does nothing but silt my clothes with red, clay-laden earth and crust my hands with heavy, rain-soaked dirt. I lunge at the heap of dirt piled by the grave, grab armfuls, and pull them on me. I'm howling like a lone coyote desperate for its pack.

At last the heap shifts, and a torrent of black crashes over me. A rock knocks my head, and I fall. I land in a muddy puddle and wait for the rest to fall.

I wait until dark, my sides heaving, my lips pouring curses, my legs shaking and bloodied. Nothing more falls. I'm too tired to care. I can't save Helen. I can't save me. I don't know if my mother lies in an undiscovered grave like this one, rotting in a state, a city, a town I don't remember. What would I do if I saw Victor again? Kill him? I don't think I have that in me, to kill someone. But I don't want to find out if that's lurking inside me, hiding behind my love of Helen and Richie and art.

I can't stay here. I have to save Richie. It's damn unlikely I'll ever find him, but I have to try.

29

JOSHUA

"May almighty God have mercy on us, . . ."

Darkness flutters at my eyelids, drawing me up and away from dreams of the saints welcoming me. I open my eyes to see Dad silhouetted against the refrigerator light, his underwear tight across his stomach but bagging pathetically over his butt. I squeeze my eyes shut. I haven't made a sound, so he doesn't know I'm awake.

He crosses to stand an arm's length from me. I can smell the jerky he's chewing and his sweat. I sense him leaning over me, then I hear Mom's footsteps.

"Let him sleep, Jacob."

"He's been sleeping for two days. Are you sure he's okay?"

Two days! But I had woken up sometime in the darkness. I'd crept into Angela's room and listened with every muscle. But I'd heard nothing.

So I'd taken her diary. Like rust eats into a car, I've eaten into my sister's mind and heart by reading her last recorded month.

He came over today, when I was alone. I didn't know why at first, but we talked for a while, then he asked me to play the piano. We laughed when I tried to play one of his requests without music and I made some awful mistakes. I didn't know he liked music.

And again:

He sang along with me today, and when he left, we kissed. Not to be trite, but I heard music.

And:

I said I was going to the movies with a friend, but I met him and we drove to see the new romantic comedy. He didn't even suggest a horror or cop movie. Just asked what I wanted to see. He smiles so much, and he's always so nice. I never thought he'd be this way. I thought I knew him, but I guess I didn't. He's so different when we're alone. I don't even try to talk to him at school because I don't want to know if he'll be the same there as he's always been or if he'll risk being himself. But he

watches me all the time, just like I watch
him. And, when no one's looking, we smile.

She hadn't written the guy's name, and I'm dying to know. I was translating the next entry when Mom's alarm had buzzed, and she stumbled across the hall to turn Angela. I stuffed the journal under the couch cushions and faked sleep.

But sleep had taken over for real.

Since I can't check the diary in front of Mom and Dad, I'll have to wait to find out who Angela loved.

"Sleep is the best thing for him. Besides, he's slept about twenty hours, not two days. Maybe he'll be over whatever he caught when he wakes up."

Dad grunts, and the springs of the La-Z-Boy creak as he drops into it. An ad for *20/20* blares. It's on next. That means it's sometime before ten on Friday. I didn't call Maggie to tell her I wouldn't be at the game. She's going to hate me. Of course, I wasn't at school either, so maybe she figured I was too sick to call.

"Josh?" Dad says, staring at me. My eyes have been open, even though I wasn't aware of it. "Are you feeling better?"

I rub my head, as if that will help me focus in the dim, blue-lit room. I'd like more light, but I don't want to turn on a lamp in case it makes me look worse. Mom's sitting on the newer sofa: the one pressed up against the dining-room table, the one that replaced Angela's piano. "I'm okay," I mutter, looking at her, hoping my eyes have cleared of angels' voices, hoping she trusts me again.

Her feet sit side by side like a pair of shoes in a neat freak's closet. Her knees are pressed together, and her hands are clutched in her lap. Is all that tension because of me? "Does your stomach feel better? Are you hungry? I can make you a sandwich," she says to the silk flowers on the table, and my heart sinks. Mom has never looked away from me before.

I have to try to eat. It's the only way she'll let me anywhere near Angela again, and I've sworn to take care of her forever. No one else will be able to protect her. Mom's not strong enough to beat Victor, and Dad isn't exactly up to it.

"Are there any chips in the house?" Dad asks.

His belly is bloated, but I don't say he doesn't need them. "I'll see." I follow Mom into the kitchen. The boom box is on the counter, and I check the CD. Bach's *High Mass*. I cringe. I pour a bowl of salt-and-vinegar chips for Dad but take none for myself. I hate them.

While I'm delivering Dad's chips, Mom pushes the play button on the CD player, and the opening notes of the *Mass* ache into the house. I falter. I hear the *Mass*'s notes echo in Angela's room—guttural moans that struggle to take form, become words. They become angelic voices, like those I'd heard in church with Andy. I shake my head. Mom's watching me, and I smile. Her eyes drop to the sandwich, but I catch a glimpse of relief in them. If I can smile, I must be returning to normal. I have to eat. I have to keep the food down.

"You're blocking the television," Dad says, his eyes riveted on a commercial.

I step out of the way. The orchestra picks up the chorus's theme when their part ends. With their silence, Angela falls silent, and I can move again. Mom hands me a sandwich, and I pass it to Dad. I grab mine and sit at the table. Why are the angelic voices singing now?

Mom sits opposite me. Her hands press against a mug of chamomile tea that sweats rings onto the table. She swabs these with her robe sleeve but says nothing. She doesn't even watch me.

God may have withdrawn, but He's sent these others. And They are peaceful, not demanding, angry, judgmental. I wish, though, that They'd chosen a different piece of music. I can't sit still through the whole *Mass*. In fact, I haven't listened to Bach's *Mass* since Angela's accident. I take a big bite of my bologna sandwich. When it doesn't set off my stomach, I devour the sandwich and make another.

"Sleep did you good, hey?" Dad says. He leans back in his chair, not looking at me, but noticing everything I do. Chip crumbs litter his chest.

A soprano has taken up a lighter movement. "I guess." I take a chance. "There was a football game tonight. A play-off game."

Dad glances at the cable box, checking the time.

"Some kids are having postgame parties. Maggie, that girl I went out with a while ago, she wants me to go. Do you think I can meet her?"

Mom's eyes lift from her tea as the soprano gives way to a mixed chorus. "I don't know, Josh. You might be better off staying home and resting."

"I'm not sleepy anymore, Mom."

Dad says, "He should go. 'Bout time he got a girlfriend. Make sure you're not out too late, though. And no drinking and driving." He grins, and for a second I see the old dad, the one who taught me to fish and play football. The one I thought would always be there for me.

Mom follows me to the hall as the trumpets begin the *Gloria*. "Josh, don't you want to shower?"

Listening to the music isn't as bad as I expected, but maybe it wasn't this section that drove me crazy before. I grind my teeth, then force a smile, the kind that always works on Mom. "I will, Mom." I dart into the bathroom, close the door, and ignore her presence on the other side. I turn the water on full blast in the sink, start the shower, flush the toilet.

But still I can hear the voices singing.

I plunge into the shower, shaking my head and ignoring the sting at the base of my skull. There aren't any parties. I don't know where I'll go, but I can't stay here. The music is nearing the point where it stopped before—for Angela and for me.

"Josh?" As I pass her in the living room, Mom stretches out her hand and strokes the bandage on the back of my head. She doesn't look like she's moved at all while I showered and dressed. "How—"

I grab my coat and the car keys, then kiss her on the cheek. "I won't be late, Mom. Promise."

I burst into the night like a freed werewolf. I suck in silence as though my lungs have been clogged with song. The living-room curtain lifts, and light seeps across the yard. I run through it, away from Mom's eyes, afraid she'll see the blackness at my core. I scramble into the car, banging both my head and my shin. Without checking for traffic, I gun the car onto the road. I hit seventy before the car reaches the flat stretch at the bottom.

But I have nowhere to go. I cruise Andy's mom's house, but

it's dark and Andy's car is gone. I screech up to his dad's, but that's dark, too. Where would he go? Did he have a date? I check the football field and find it empty except for the cleanup crew and a few parents arguing over the coach's tactics. Hesitating between the stands, I jingle my keys while I decide where to check next.

He finds me there.

"Been looking for you," Victor says in my ear, and I regret driving like a maniac through town. He probably saw me and came after me, thinking I was cracking.

Well, I'm not. "Why are you looking for me?" I say.

"You weren't at school."

"So? I slept. Is that a crime?" But I've missed so much school since Helen's death. I jingle my keys again.

Victor nods and snatches them. I didn't even see his hand move. "Let's go for a ride."

I follow because there's nothing else to do. I sit in the passenger seat because there's nowhere else to sit. I wonder, briefly, how God would want me to handle my situation.

Give me a chance to fix my mistakes, to put things right so Angela can come back, I plead. I wait for a response, but none comes.

We leave the park. The houses slip by, then flash like a strobe as we shoot through town, past McDonald's and the handful of kids leaning against their cars outside the bowling alley. That's where I spot Andy's car. I twist and see its lights come on. It pulls onto the road behind us.

"Shit," Victor mutters. He shoves the gas to the floor. "Asshole voted himself your protector, didn't he?"

"Do I need protecting?"

Victor grins in the light of the last of the streetlamps. "What do you think? We're going for a few beers?"

"Why don't you get off my back?" I ask, suddenly hard, remembering Angela. "I've done nothing wrong."

He steers the car at a tree, then pulls it back onto the road at the last second. "Scared, pussy?"

Song floods the car. The angelic voices start on Bach's *Gloria*, move to the *Benedictus*. I am not alone. I meet Victor's eye. "No, I don't believe I am."

His eyes narrow. He grips the wheel like he's ringing a quail's neck. "You should be."

"Why, because you did a chickenshit thing like throw a firebomb at a girl's house?" Bach's lyrics speak of glory and eternal life. The angels move on to the *Halleluia*. I'm on the right track.

"No, because I'm going to kill you."

He says it like he means it, like he's enforcing the six-pack bet he made with Andy, but he doesn't know me and what I'm capable of. He thinks it'll be easy to silence me. But what he thinks, what everyone assumes, isn't the truth. They don't know what I carry in my heart or the way my pledge burned itself into my soul and changed who I am. They don't know why I made that pledge. They think I'm the sappy religious fanatic, the kid who says he wants to be a priest. I grin, knowing I look like Victor did a moment ago. The chorus sings of the Resurrection and the end of death in triumph and joy. I connect the dots from Victor and his threats, to my destroyed shrine, to where we're going. "You ruined my church," I say as we zoom toward the top of Denton Hill.

"Church, my ass. It was easy to ruin and stupid to build. You're a weirdo."

Weirdo or believer? I'd rather be either one than a creep like Victor. "The meek shall inherit the earth," I whisper.

"Your sister was a goody two-shoes like you. Too good for the likes of me. Or for that matter, any guy." He smirks.

I force my hands to stay flat on my thighs. I will not sink to his level, although I long to smash his face into the windshield. Besides, I don't get why he's talking about Angela like this. Threats to kill her, yeah, but that she was different, better than everyone, no. "Leave my sister out of this. She's comatose, not a goody two-shoes," I say.

"She wasn't always," he says. "She used to be a real person." His use of past tense hits me like a kick to the kidneys.

"She still is," I say reflexively, protectively. I don't want Victor dirtying Angela with his insinuations. "She could come out of it."

"Yeah, and I could win the Heisman. Get real. She's dying. My mom said so. Can't sit up anymore, can't breathe on her own. Every day she's weaker."

If Victor knows Angela's dying, then the whole town knows. Even still, I don't have to admit it. That would mean I've lost all faith.

The voices continue to sing, although I don't recognize what. They've left the strains of Bach's *Mass* and are improvising. With their improvisation, my certainty fades. Has my suppressed rage pushed God away? Does He expect me to accept my fate or fight back? The car jounces along a rutted drive, and fear seizes my guts. I can't die like this. I'd leave Angela unprotected. I jump out as soon as the car stops.

"Now," says Victor, "let's go for a little walk."

"A little drive, a little walk. Then what?" I don't move, buying time for Andy to catch up.

"Then a little fight, and one of us walks back."

I laugh.

He swings to glare at me. His taut arms whip around, and his clenched fists ram into his sides. He steps closer. His eyes almost vanish. "You're crazy," he says. "Ef-ing crazy, like your sister."

"She was sane," I say. "Saner than anyone I know. She had dreams, though. She wanted out of this hellhole, and she'd have made it. People can't stand that, especially the ones who are afraid of leaving."

"Then why was she seeing me? She had one tight pussy."

I shatter. Angela hadn't written the guy's name in her diary. Could she have been seeing Victor? His ugly face leers into mine.

I shake my head. "I don't believe it. She'd never date you." She hated jerks like Victor, although she hadn't mentioned him when she ran down other guys in her journal.

Victor hits me hard in the jaw. "She would, and she did," he says.

I trip on a branch and land in rattling leaves, which give way to slime. I skitter back as he plunges after me.

"And she was no virgin!" he bellows. "She was the best lay I ever had. Come on! I want this to look like self-defense! Fight me!"

I fly at him, my world colorless with rage. "Take it back!" I scream. "Take it back!" I go for his throat, but he grabs my wrist, twists me to the left, and drops me to the ground.

He laughs, cold and biting. It knifes my gut. He leans over and kicks me in the ribs with his infamous boots. Something gives, pain crushes me from skin to organs. But he doesn't follow up the kick. He straightens. "What a wuss. That all you got? They better teach priests some self-defense or something, or you'll be mugged and murdered."

THIS IS YOUR CROSS, the Voice says. HOW WILL YOU BEAR IT? WILL YOU BECOME LIKE HIM OR FOLLOW MY SON?

"I used to light a cigarette when I finished screwing her," Victor says. He leans in closer to me, mimes smoking. "When I was done with it, I'd stub it out on her ass. If you were home, you could check for the scars, but you'll never get to now."

I shake my head, struggle with the rage that gorges my throat. *He's lying. Keep calm.*

But I can't. Anger, humiliation, and grief win. I falter, and the Voice goes quiet.

I thrash out with my legs to trip him, but Victor dances sideways, as though he knew I would try that. I scrabble away. When I am far enough back, I flip over and stand. I raise my arms, clench my teeth against the blow I plan to deliver and the one I wait to receive, and turn to face him. But my flailing arms connect with nothing. Bewildered, I open my eyes.

Someone leaps from the shadows onto Victor's back. Victor's legs buckle, and he grunts, "What the hell?" He grabs at his assailant, shredding clothing like tissue paper before he finds a solid grip and drags his attacker to the ground. Fists and knees thrust. Legs tangle, and curses fly.

"Andy!" I rush toward the struggling figures, grab the one on top by the hair, and yank. Victor's glittering, slitted eyes stare at me as I pull his head back. A moment later an elbow smashes into my gut, rekindling the pain in my side. I double over like a collapsing balloon.

"Stay out of this, Josh!" Andy jumps away from Victor. Both are breathing hard. "It's me you're really after, Victor. Just admit it's me you want!" Andy circles Victor.

Victor rubs his chin. He doesn't take his eyes off Andy. "He's going to tell. He's driving around like a maniac. He's losing weight, missing school, sitting in on the wrong classes. He's drawing attention to himself. They know, man! They'll ask him two questions, and he'll break."

"Like burning someone's house isn't suspicious?"

Victor lunges, pummels Andy one-two in the face, but Andy punches him in the gut. Victor bends, and Andy brings both hands, clutched together in a massive fist, down on Victor's back. Unbelievably, Victor stays upright.

Tag-team him. Don't let him catch his breath, I think. I dart forward to kick Victor in the ass, but Victor catches my foot and flips me. Pain splits my side when I hit the ground.

But Victor can't finish the job. Andy hits him hard in the left eye, then slams his left fist into Victor's neck. Victor flails with both arms and catches Andy hard in the chest and neck. Andy falls.

I force my weight onto my trembling legs. I have to protect Andy. I stagger forward as Victor straddles Andy. Something glints in his hand, and the familiar bile of fear chokes me. I fling myself at Victor like a tree frog flies at a tree. But Andy's brings up his knee, quick and vicious, and Victor's rolling away. I land on the ground, squeezing into a ball to keep from hurting myself. Andy pulls me to my feet.

Victor's already up, although he's swaying and cupping his balls. His eyes are wide, dangerous, unlike anything I've ever seen.

"Oh my God!" I say between ragged breaths.

"Wouldn't hurt if you said a few prayers," Andy says. His hint of laughter is out of place. One of his eyes is swelling shut, and the other has a gash bleeding into it. The bandage I put on his cheek is gone, and his cut gapes. He clutches his side, but I don't think Victor caught him with his rib-breaking boots.

Dread pours into me like water into a submerging bucket. This won't end with three guys alive. "We have to get out of here."

But Andy's almost as maddened as Victor. "Have to finish this first," he says. "He can't keep doing crap like this. Somebody has to stop him."

Victor stalks us, growling. He mutters Angela's name again and again, as if it's a threat we have to respond to.

My temper rises.

But Andy only laughs. "You may have wanted her, asshole, but you never had her. I should know." He winks at me. And I understand the wink, the diary, this fight. But before I can react, Andy's head slams back as Victor crashes into him. Victor's fists are blurs, bruising Andy's sides, cracking his ribs and the sides of Andy's head.

This fight isn't about Helen and whether I'll tell or not. I think of Victor using that date-rape drug on girls. Had he tried it on Angela, and Andy stopped him? Such knight-in-shining-armor stuff was what Angela wanted. Had he saved Angela but never told me?

The thought of Victor raping my sister sends me beyond rage. I shred Victor's shirt, trying to drag him from Andy. I tear fistfuls of hair from his head while he swings it from side to side like a crazed bull. I throw punches at his head and sides. My left fist sinks into his eye, and the way it gives makes my stomach turn. My thumb slides out, and I'm pressing, pressing into the softness of his socket, ignoring Victor's bellows. He rears and lets go of Andy. Both of his arms come around like dinosaur tails to slash at me.

Andy staggers around us, yelling, "Let go, Joshie. Let me in there!"

Victor thrusts at me with the knife, but Andy grabs his hand before it connects with my neck. Darkness oozes between his fingers.

My hands clutch, gouge, dig into Victor. My teeth find flesh, and I taste blood. I scream and sob. I shrug off Andy's attempts to pull me from Victor. Victor's fists pummel every inch of me that he can reach. My legs go mushy, and my arms burn from wrist to shoulder.

Only when he crushes me against a tree do I let go. Then his weight is gone. His feet thunder away, and I collapse to the ground. Heaving breaths ravage my lungs. I can barely raise my head. Andy dances around Victor, just out of reach. He's buying me time to pick myself up. I force my arms to push me up and my legs to support me. When I'm swaying but upright, Andy yells, "Get in the car, Joshie. Lock yourself in."

But I don't. I stagger toward them, wondering at Andy's lightness as I watch the blood course down his arm and drip off his fingers in the eery whitewashed light illuminating our battle.

Victor lunges again, misses Andy by an inch. Andy slows, tempts him, slides glances my way. His concern for me gives Victor openings, and he thrusts the knife into each one. Andy dodges each attempt to kill him by a smaller and smaller margin. I have to help.

I move behind Victor, who's snorting and swearing. "I'll kill you and him then," he grunts. He rakes the air between him and Andy with the long knife. I can barely stuff a breath into my lungs because of the pain in my chest and side. Still, I circle. He has to have a weakness, a way for me to end this. His muscled arms swing with precision, ripple with strength. There is no weakness there. His near-naked chest heaves, but not as badly as mine or Andy's. Desperate, I study his feet. He lumbers forward, lifts one foot as he plunges his knife toward Andy. For an instant, before he plants his foot again, he's standing on only one leg.

One leg. If only I could jerk it out from under him as he goes for Andy. If only Andy could hold on while I find the chance. But Andy's weakening. Each time Victor moves, Andy's response is slower.

But I have to wait. *Hold on, Andy,* I pray. *Hold on.*

When Victor lunges again, I kick his supporting leg with everything I have left. Nothing happens. Andy's face hovers beyond Victor's broad shoulder. *He won't fall,* I think. *I'm too weak. We're going to die.*

Then Victor's raised leg lands on my other leg, and he stumbles. Like a sawn-through tree, he groans and plummets. Victor crashes to the ground.

I'm on my feet before I can think. I leap after Victor as he tumbles downhill, and I land on his back. I jump up and down, slam his head into the dirt, kick, dance, and scream, "Don't ever, ever say stuff like that about my sister!" My words echo through the woods, rebound, and drive me on. "She was perfect. A saint. If you touched her, I'll kill you!"

Victor's hands grab for my flying feet, then he tries to push his ass up.

"Grab the knife!" I yell at Andy, who moves as though he's more afraid of me than of Victor.

"I don't see it." He shuffles through leaf litter and dirt, sending grit and grime into Victor's face.

"Get off," Victor moans. I can barely hear him.

But I laugh. "Not until Andy has the knife." I dance faster and faster. My feet grind his flesh, mush it into bruises, crush his lies into dust.

He groans, flails, beats the ground. He wails in agony and defeat.

I've beaten him! Joy and the high of victory surge into my body and mind. I've never beaten a guy before, and now, with Andy's help, I've whipped the toughest guy in school.

Andy scuffles over on hands and knees. I look for the elation in his face, but see only puzzlement. His hands dart quicker, but don't touch Victor. Victor's hands barely move. They look like dead kittens in the dirt.

Andy leans back, stares at me. His eyes could burn holes in the night sky. "Let him up, Josh," he says. He holds out a hand caked with mud. "Now!"

I stop dancing and step off Victor.

Victor rolls onto his side, a moan his only protest. On the ground, the knife handle glints in the light of a billion stars. No blade is visible.

But from a slit in Victor's chest where the blade rests, blood flows. A bubble, dark and glinting, grows between Victor's lips, pops. His breath rattles, gurgles in and out, in and out, in and out. Slower, slower, slower.

It's what we were fighting for. It's what we wanted.

Still, Andy screams, "Oh my God! Oh my God!"

"It was self-defense, an accident! He's not dead yet." I crouch, but I can't touch him to check. "I'll get help." I sprint for the cabin, only to smash into blackness.

30

MICHAEL

"Truly, he shall be returned intact."

I'm on the Grabbits' cabin porch when the first set of car lights jounces down the pitted driveway. I huddle lower. Christ, all I wanted was to say good-bye, and now I'll probably be busted for breaking and entering. I ease the newly picked door shut, not locking it in case they go away. I fade into the woods.

But the car stops halfway to the cabin, and two guys climb out. I can tell from the way they stand and move that they're arguing, throwing out their chests and arms along with their anger. I catch words, but not the sense of what they're saying. A second car eases into the driveway with its lights off, its driver obviously familiar with the twists and ruts. It stops as the two figures clash, and the skinnier one is tossed aside like a sack of feathers.

It's not a fair fight, but I don't feel like evening the odds. I have enough crap on my plate.

But someone else doesn't feel the same way I do. He hops out of his car and crashes into the big guy like he intends to kill him. He goes down but pops back up before I can exhale. More posturing, more words, more blows, then the newest guy goes after the big guy, only to be knocked to the ground. He kicks up, sending the moose backward, clutching his crotch and groaning.

They hesitate, and I can feel their breath stirring the night, raising the scent of the dead. They're serious about this. Someone's going to get hurt. I move out of hiding, but none of them sees me slipping from tree to tree. The big guy jumps the middle-sized guy, going for his throat. But then the skinny guy goes berserk, nearly making me run away. I don't want to be a part of this, but somehow I am.

When the little guy is thrown off and the other two are circling, I almost call out, but before I do, the little guy trips the monster who's lunging with a knife.

A chill shakes me. That must be the guy who killed Helen. I run, wanting a piece of him, too. But the skinny guy's dancing on the big guy's back, whose groans are growing fainter and fainter.

By the time the guy jumps off the monster, even I, fifty yards away, know it's too late.

"I'll get help!" echoes through the woods. The kid sprints for the house, but in his panic, he slams into a big oak. He flips like he's doing a back layover and lies still.

So it's me who runs for the house, ignoring the remaining guy's sobs and screams, finding the phone and dialing 911. It's me who brings ice from the fridge. It's me who finds Andy Grabbit cradling Josh Stedman.

"He didn't do anything wrong," Andy yells at me, at the world. "He had no part in this."

But I saw his leg snake out and take the big guy down. I saw his triumphant dance on the back of evil. I press the ice against Josh's head, which has grown a huge welt near his temple. That's bad. I nod toward the body in the driveway. "And him?"

"Victor?" Andy watches me. He won't let me take Josh off his lap. "Victor was insane. He wanted to kill Josh because he thought he was going to tell." He stops, goes white.

"Tell?" My heart freezes.

"Yeah, tell." He sounds resigned, yet afraid.

"About?" I'm cold, dead inside. I want rage. I want fury. Instead, I have the sinking feeling that knowing who isn't going to help the *what*. I will always be without Helen. I meet Andy's eye. His fear is real, as is his grief and pain.

He looks at me long and hard. He touches Josh's shoulder. His face softens, and he almost smiles. "He's pretty damn tough underneath, you know? But he didn't have anything to do with it, all right?" Andy's voice hardens, and his face stiffens. He's challenging me.

I want to run, to scream, to drown out his words. I don't really want to know. When it was Victor, I could stand it. He was brutal, bullying, mean, but Andy or Josh? Andy is stupid and a show-off, but not mean. And Josh? He's, well, good, sweet.

Like ghosts in the air, Helen says, "It's not right," and Moshie says, "Sometimes, something is nothing more than a stupid mistake, done without thought."

Andy's hand grabs my wrist. "All right?" he demands.

I nod as tears make it impossible to see. There will be no vindication for Helen.

"We were there when Helen died."

"All of you?" I choke.

"Yeah. But Josh didn't do anything. He wanted to call the cops from the start. He was like his sister, good, you know." He bends over Josh, says something I can't catch. I think it's something about fixing his buddy up.

A thin wail rises far down the valley.

Andy's head comes up. "You called for help?"

"Yeah. Who killed Helen?"

His once-handsome face is battered and bloodied, but the fear is gone from his eyes. Only a hopelessness lives there now. "I did. It was an accident," he whispers. "I didn't know the gun was loaded, and I didn't know she was there—where she came from. We were alone. I was screwing with Josh's mind and showing off my dad's gun. I didn't mean for it to go off, but my finger must have slipped or the safety came off. Something. I didn't know she was hit. I swear. And it was Victor who said we had to hide her. I would've listened to Josh if Victor hadn't been there. Victor burned Shelly's house, too. He was going to kill us. I swear—" He stops, looks at Josh. "I swear to God."

The siren howls up the hill, slows, finds the driveway, but can't come up to where we are because of the parked cars.

"Don't tell them Josh did anything." Andy clutches me. "I'll take the blame. Tell them I killed Victor. Tell them that Victor was trying to kill Josh, and I saved him."

An accident. No murderer to punish. No one to blame. Hell, I'd brought her to the party. If I hadn't done that, she'd be alive.

Andy's grip tightens on my arm. I meet his eye. I have to do what Helen would want. I'm shaking, but I say, "But that's the truth. I saw it all. That's what happened."

"Are you sure?" Andy whispers. "Because I don't know

what's right and wrong anymore. I don't know what the truth is."
His eyes look odd, unfocused.

Then they snap back as a voice calls, "Found one here."

Andy and I stare at each other, wait in the silence that follows.
"He's dead."

Andy's eyes drop. He touches Josh's cheek. "Promise me,
Michael. He did nothing wrong."

"I promise," I say, then stand. "Over here," I yell. "My
friend's buddy is pretty badly hurt."

The police arrive first, followed by a paramedic crew and an
ambulance. They load Josh on a stretcher, then help Andy into
the ambulance. They leave Victor for later. Andy's talking fast as
the officers eye me, then him. He tells them everything in a rapid
staccato that leaves them no opportunity to question dirt-
encrusted me.

I watch them go, then turn to the cabin. But an officer, his
voice soft, familiar, says, "There's nothing there for you,
Michael. I'll take you to her grave if you'd like."

I stare. He doesn't suspect me. "I kind of messed up where
they buried her," I say. I sob, then stuff my tears inside.

He gives a mirthless laugh. "I figured." He taps my clothes.
Then, when I'm buckled into the front seat, he says, "You need
stitches, too."

I touch my forehead. "Had a fight with a rock."

He nods. "Yeah." He drives me to the cemetery, but she's not
there, either. She's nowhere. In a rush, when I forgave Andy, the
fleeting images of her that have haunted me since her death vanished. I'm left with air, loneliness.

My knees sag against the headstone, but no tears come. She's gone. I'm empty. I hug myself and rock, my fingers finding a lump of material in my pocket. Her sock. I kiss it, fold it, and tuck it back into my pants when my tears have stopped. At last, I stand and walk to the policeman's car.

It isn't until the car's light comes on and he adjusts his seat belt that I realize we graduated together. "Hey, Gabe," I say. "Didn't know you were a cop."

He smiles. "Yeah."

I wait, but what's he going to say to me? *I didn't know you were a messed-up idiot?*

At the hospital, they let me shower and give me a gown. I only need a few stitches. They admit me anyway, probably because they don't know I have anyplace to go. It's okay, though. I don't want to be alone.

When I'm in my room, Gabe returns. "You need anything?"

I almost smile. "Some clothes." I tell him where I've been staying. As he leaves, I ask, "You ever been to Montana?"

"Naw. Never went farther than police training down near Harrisburg. Someday maybe. You heading there?"

"Maybe."

"Hey." He hesitates, then plunges on. "I knew you didn't do it. Told the sheriff that. Nobody who draws like you or treats their girl like you did could do that."

He's gone before I can answer.

31

JOSHUA

". . . forgive us our sins, . . ."

It's the light that draws me back. It dangles in sparkling panels. Rainbows and colored beams dance through my fogged brain.

It's also a voice, relentless in what it's telling the dark figure beside him. "He had nothing to do with it," it says. "Victor was going to kill him. When I saw Victor driving Josh's car, I knew something was up, so I followed them. But Josh had nothing to do with Victor's death."

Victor's dead?

"We understand that. Why don't you sit quietly? You need to relax." The figure shoves the voice away, then bends over me. "Pupils are responsive," the figure says, relieved.

I drift, wandering through realms of glory and beauty.

The voice pulls me, making me stay below that dangling lamp. "No, I won't leave him. Take me with him."

PEACE IS REACHABLE. JUST LET GO.

"It would be better for you to go in the second ambulance.

He's coding again." I don't know who this is, but I want them to go away.

"For who?" barks the voice. "You? Me? Not for Josh!"

"Pupils responsive—barely." That's a woman near my head. What's she doing? My eyelids flutter.

"Listen, Josh," says the voice. "I'm going to tell them everything. Everything, you hear? You're not responsible, okay? Come back. You didn't do anything wrong. Victor got what he deserved."

AND HELEN?

I moan. I don't want to hear Him.

An accident, I say.

WHAT ABOUT ANGELA?

Ah, Angela. Bless us, O Lord, for these Thy gifts, which we are about to receive, through the bounty of Christ, Our Lord, Amen. Angela. She was playing Bach. Over and over and over. High Mass. B Minor. *It was Bach, really.*

BACH? ONLY BACH?

Yes, Bach! She wouldn't stop playing it. I asked her over and over to quit. I had to study. I had a chem final.

"But my teacher wants me to learn the organ part by heart. I have to listen to it. Why don't you study outside? By the pond?"

"He's coding again!" Hands hold me to a metal table.

"I'll show you what can go into the pond!"

Oh, Angela, I didn't mean you.

"Give it back, Josh! I need it!"

The slickness of the disk in my fingers, the crack of the jewel case as I put the disk with its mate. A two-CD set, a classic, a masterpiece.

Annoying crap is what it was.

She chased me. I shrugged her off. I wasn't so good, so nonviolent then.

The pond was high, cold with the spring melt, but it wasn't impossibly deep. I could wade out, swim across in about seventeen strokes. Not as many as the length of the town pool takes. I threw the case hard at the pipe in the center of the pond, sucking the water out of the pond, like lips at an over-full cup. I watched the case float there a moment, then turned to her.

"*Now I can have some peace and quiet.*"

"*Josh! I can't afford another. I need it. Go get it, please. You're a better swimmer.*"

"*It's not deep. Get it yourself if you need it so bad. Should have listened when I told you to quit playing the damn thing.*"

IS THAT ALL?

What?

ALL THAT HAPPENED?

I went into the house. I studied for chemistry. I was there when Dad came home from work, started screaming.

YOU DIDN'T HEAR HER GO INTO THE WATER?

Why should I?

YOU DIDN'T HEAR HER STRUGGLE?

No.

YOU DIDN'T NOTICE THE RISING WATER?

I didn't look out. I didn't know the pipe could be plugged, that if it was, the water would rise to fill the whole basin! It's spring-fed, plus the snow was melting. The water poured in, but it couldn't pour out. How was I to know the plastic case would plug the hole? How was I

*to know she'd be stupid enough to jump in, swim after it? I'd have
bought her another disk! I just wanted some peace and quiet to study.*

DID YOU FIND YOUR PEACE AND QUIET?

"Andy?"

"I'm here, buddy, I'm here. They're letting me ride with you.
Then I'll give them my formal statement. Everything's okay,
buddy. It's all right."

"Angela?"

"Angela? She's at your house. She's okay."

"No, I killed Angela."

"It was Victor, buddy. Angela wasn't there."

"Voices, Andy. The Voices say I killed her."

"No, Josh, you didn't."

"Helen?"

"Not her, either."

"Don't cry, Andy. You didn't mean it."

"I know. I know."

PEACE CAN ONLY BE FOUND AFTER PENANCE.

Cold circles press against my chest. "Pupils unresponsive.
Heart rate flat. Stand clear."

"How many times are you going to do that?"

"As many times as it takes, son. We don't understand it. He
hit that tree hard, but not this hard. He should have snapped out
of it long ago."

"Will he be the same?"

"This doesn't hurt him."

"No, but the lack of oxygen, the concussion? Will that damage him? He's my best friend. He was sweet, you know. He

loved his sister so much. He was always taking care of her. You don't find too many guys like that."

"Heart rate normal. Pupils responsive."

"Is he back for good?"

"Let's hope so." A jolt, the flash of colors, footsteps, and sobs. "Ah, in here, Mrs. Stedman. He's doing better. He's almost stable."

32

MICHAEL

77: "Understanding others is knowledge,
Understanding oneself is enlightenment . . ."

I expect the opening door to reveal Gabe with my stuff. He is, after all, the only person who knows I'm in the hospital.

At first, the widening rectangle shows only the hallway's bright light. It's night, and my head throbs, more from crying than from the stitches. Then the door stops, and a hand, tentative and shaking, touches the door frame.

Helen's hand?

I blink fast, hard, but my vision only blurs.

Then she steps forward, head sagging, shoulders hunched. She wears a dark coat I've seen dozens of times. But it's not Helen.

It's her mother.

My stomach clenches. Why has she come? Does she want to accuse me of taking Helen to the place of her death? To say I'm as guilty as Andy?

She hesitates. Shadows mask her face.

I cringe, but she doesn't speak. Does she know that Andy

confessed and Josh is in critical condition? Has she found out about Victor's death already?

It was her daughter who was killed. She'd be one of the first to know. Someone—an ambulance driver, nurse, technician, police officer—someone has told her who killed her daughter. I can see it in the frightened way she stands.

But can she believe I'm innocent after weeks of believing I was guilty? The whole time I dated Helen, her family was against me. I can't imagine them forgetting their hatred. My guts tremble on the verge of diarrhea.

"Michael?" Her voice peeps into the room like the tiny pond frogs that serenade spring. "Are you sleeping?"

Why is she afraid? What possible harm can I do her? Doesn't she know that she has the larger weapon? She could shatter my image of Helen, tell me that she hated me, that she had promised to dump me, that the party was supposed to have been our last date.

"No," I choke. My body stinks of chemicals and fear. *Don't take her from me. Don't condemn me. Don't leave me with nothing.*

"I'm sorry to disturb you." She comes into the room, her face white in the center of her daffodil yellow hair. Helen's had been a natural gold, but Mrs. Mitchell uses dye. Her feet are stuffed into rubber-soled boots that silence her footsteps. When the door falls shut behind her, she jumps like a finch at a feeder.

She startles again when I turn on the light behind my head. Her face is sallow, shrunken, wrinkled. Her resemblance to Helen is lost in the torrent of grief I know too well. Her hands clutch a box, and her whole body curls around it as though protecting either it or herself.

"I was awake," I say. "You didn't disturb me."

Her eyes swim the gulf between us. "You look so different," she says at last. "So—so marked. Thinner," she adds.

I nod, but I don't tell her how she looks. Helen wouldn't have wanted me to. She would have said to take care of her, to go easy on her.

She shuffles forward. "I shouldn't have come—"

I can't help groaning. I turn away. Here it comes. She's going to accuse me of being responsible for Helen's death, for stealing her daughter from her.

"No, no!" She rushes to the foot of my bed. "It's not like that. I don't deserve to ask you to forgive me. Us." Her voice breaks. She stops, draws a ragged breath. "We shouldn't have thought you had—"

She can't say it, and I can't help her. Disbelief at what she's saying has taken my breath.

"I knew you loved Helen. It was frightening, though, to see how much you cared for each other. I had such dreams for her. She was so different. Brilliant, like a light, you know?"

"Yeah." I can't look at her. I want to say, *I'll live in the dark forever,* but I can tell she knows that, too.

"I didn't want to lose her light or see it shuttered someplace where it wouldn't be seen."

"And I'd do that to her." Bitterness seeps beneath my anguish.

"No, you wouldn't have. But I might have. I smothered her. I kept her safe at all costs. So she had to slip away, sneak, run from me into the very danger I tried to keep her from. If only I had let her go. If only I had told my husband that you should be allowed to date her. If only I had let you work in our basement or visit us. If only I had—"

"Stood between her and the bullet?"

Her head jerks. Her grief is so intense, she has no tears.

"It's where I'd stand," I say. "Over and over, I put myself there, between her and that gun. But I can't change—" My fists clench. I punch the bed. "I can't change it!"

"Oh, Michael, none of us can." She touches my foot, and the package falls onto the bed.

"That doesn't stop me wanting it." With every breath, with every heartbeat, with every thought, I wish it.

"But you have a life ahead of you," she says. "Helen would never have wanted you to give up. She used to show me your paintings, when we were alone. She was so proud of you, and I know enough about art to tell that you are good. You mustn't stop painting, Michael. You have to continue for Helen. She believed in you. I'm not sure she believed in anything else, but she did in you."

This is a gift. I have to accept it, even if the beautiful wrapping covers an empty package. I have Helen's belief, but not Helen.

"I can't draw anymore," I mutter, scrunching up like Richie used to do when he was mad or frightened. "I only draw nightmare pictures of eyes and hands reaching to me, begging for help."

"You can draw." She bends over the package and unties the string holding it shut.

I don't want to see what she pulls out. There's no hope. I'm alone, lost. Fatherless, motherless, brotherless, loverless. What good can my artistic ability do? "Don't." I turn away.

She ignores me. "She would have wanted me to give you these. I understand that you don't have much since . . . The police said you probably don't have a picture of Helen."

I don't want a picture. I want Helen.

She turns a photo to me. It's not the one in the paper, and she must see the relief in my eyes. "We didn't give them our favorite picture for that. It would have left us with nothing, you know?" The crack in her shell widens, and she blinks rapidly.

In this picture, Helen is laughing. In the other, she'd had a small, knowing smile. Almost as if she had figured out the secret of the universe. But in this one, she's laughing at some joke, her niece's antics, or a puppy's playfulness. "She always wanted a dog," I say.

"I know," Mrs. Mitchell says, and again, there's a catch, a sense that she recognizes her failures. "He doesn't know I've come," she adds. "So don't tell anyone. I brought some other things, too. Stuff she'd want you to have." Her hands fly from the box as though it holds snapping turtles. She stuffs them into the crooks of her elbows, begins to back out.

"Wait!" I cry. There's so much I want to ask, and once she's gone, I'll never have another chance. She'll vanish from my life, like Helen did. I want to ask when Helen first walked and what her first word was. I want to ask, *What was she like when she was four? Five? Ten?* We never had those talks where the family tells you all the embarrassing, cute stuff about your girlfriend. We never had any talks.

"Good-bye, Michael," she says. Her feet slide toward the door as though it's too difficult to pick them off the floor. "Forgive me."

Then she bolts like a deer frightened from its bed. Her eyes look panicky, and I try to soothe her before she's gone. "I do," I call. "Forgive me?"

But she's gone.

I stare at the box a long time before I pull it toward me. Inside is the picture, several paintings I gave Helen, some letters I sent her, the things I bought her with the money I earned from my painting. In despair I lift memory after memory from the box, hoping for the key, the insight into the Helen. I was cheated of that. But these things only remind me of us, or myself. They do not evoke Helen.

On the bottom rests a pile of photocopies. The ink is smudged, and I set them on the bed beside me. They're probably report cards. Empty grades to shore up an empty heart.

I sink my head to my chest. I am beyond crying, beyond caring. I've lost Helen forever.

33

JOSHUA

"... and bring us to everlasting life."

I've lain here for hours, days. My family comes and goes. All but Angela. She's home, hanging in there, as Dad puts it when he can bring himself to speak. He doesn't say anything about Helen or Victor. Mostly he sits by the window and stares at the sky, which has taken on winter's dreariness early.

Mom flutters in, always sunny, as if she can beat the weather and the somberness of my room. A few cards are taped to the walls, but most kids haven't sent anything or called. No one, not even Maggie, has visited. What did I expect?

I haven't talked. It must be killing Mom to have two mute children who've nearly died. But I can't bring myself to say anything. What's there to say? I'm sorry?

Not that they know about Angela. That story lodges in my throat and blocks the truth everyone waits to hear. Expectation burns in their eyes. "How could you do this? How did you get involved?" What do I say? It all started one afternoon when

Angela wouldn't quit playing Bach? Or did it start at the party, when I couldn't find a way around Victor and Andy to call the police? Or had it started with my friendship with Andy?

In that case, when will it end?

A shrink came to see me. She gave me pills for depression and the auditory hallucinations the EMTs and emergency-room doctors told her about. Today the nurse delivered them just as Father Paul arrived, and he watched to be sure I took them.

But when the nurse leaves, the silence enfolds me, allowing me to slip away to a place where I can forget everything. I pretend I'll have a life when I return to school, Shelly won't hate me, and Maggie will go out with me again. Andy will be there.

Father Paul's eyes pour questions into the emptiness of my soul. "Moping won't make you feel better," he says.

I turn my head to the racing clouds, watch their ugly progress across the sky.

"You have to face what you have and haven't done." His fingers close around mine. Then, although I try not to watch what he's doing, he draws his stole from his bag, kisses it, and puts it around his neck. He sits beside me awhile, his lips moving like a baby's in sleep as he prays.

To whom? For what?

"I confess to Almighty God," Father Paul says. He takes my hand and nods at me. "And to you, my brothers and sisters."

My lips, wooden with silence, splinter and split. The prayer's rhythm invades my head. I can't not say it. But when I finally force my voice to join Father Paul's, it only whispers. "That I have sinned through my own fault."

I can't go further. So much was my fault. Helen's death, her burial, her parents' pain, Michael's loss—these are my fault. Victor's death. Angela. All of it. My fault.

The whispered trickle flows into a gush of pain, a torrent of recriminations. "I killed them both," I sob, "or I as good as did. Andy didn't mean to shoot Helen, but it's far worse that we buried her like that. Without telling, without admitting what happened. I should have called the police the minute I got home, but he said he'd kill me, my family. I should have known the police wouldn't have let Victor hurt us. They'd have arrested him or something. Or put us into protective custody."

I clutch my cracked ribs as though pain is my penance. "I shouldn't have done that to Helen's mother and father. I know how my parents hurt over Angela. No one should have to go through that. And Michael. What did all this do to him? How can I ever expect any of them to forgive me? Besides, if I'd told, Victor would be alive. I hated him, but I didn't mean to kill him. The knife was in his hand when he fell. How was I to know it'd land point up under him? That the handle would break off, leaving the blade buried in him? He was trying to kill us. Me especially, and he was saying things."

I choke, sob. "About Angela. Lies, but they pissed me off. He said he screwed her, but she would never do that with him. I fought him to keep him from ruining her reputation."

I burrow into the pillow as I wail, "She doesn't have much left. He had no right to take that, too! I'm the one who knocked him down. I didn't mean for him to land on the knife." I stop, then continue, quieter, "At that moment, though, I wanted him to be dead."

Something eases in me with my confession, but I'm still encased in guilt. I need forgiveness and don't know how to find it. I need Angela's forgiveness, but she's gone beyond my reach. I sit bolt upright, face Father Paul. I have to see the disgust in his eyes.

Father Paul clutches my hands, his wide eyes containing nothing that I expected. No hatred. No horror. No shock. Only acceptance, love, and kindness.

My defiant anger fades. I say, "I can never be like you, Father Paul, and I want to so bad. I have to put this right somehow." I feel this not because of my vow—that was panic, bargaining—but because I want to give someone the gift of love that Father Paul has given me. But I don't know if I have that strength.

I collapse, facedown, into my pillow. Father Paul's hand moves to my head. His fingers trace the cross in my tangled, dirty hair, and he says, "You have suffered so much, Josh. I accept your confession and your penance. Go, and sin no more. Will you say the Act of Contrition with me?"

I struggle out of bed. We kneel before the blowing clouds with their load of rain. I say the words. I feel the wash as drops fall, but it isn't rain. It's my tears. Father Paul cries, too, but he will never know that I cry for Angela. I haven't told him that I can hear her, moaning and begging for release. She's trapped in the body I destroyed, held prisoner and in pain.

And I hear her every thought. Day and night, my penance is to know her agony, to watch her die from the inside. It shatters me, divides me, burns me, but I can't escape. Sometimes I believe I am insane. If I say more than what I have to Father Paul, I will never be allowed out of this hospital.

I pray for her release. Which means Angela will die, but I'm not sure that's wrong. Maybe I kept her here. Maybe I forced her into a fate worse than death. It's all my fault.

But it won't be long now.

Father Paul hugs me, consoles me, tells me I am forgiven.

She can't last long.

34

MICHAEL

"Conquering others is power,
Conquering oneself is strength. . . ."

In my dream, I'm in Dad's pickup and he's following in a tank. He's madder than a terrorist, and I'm almost pissing myself I'm so scared. But Richie's with me, and I won't slow down even on the narrow, pitted roads in the back end of nowhere where we live. I swerve around a corner, taking it at almost sixty, and he's there, impossibly, in front of me. I slam on the brakes and throw it in reverse, but as I do, I see Helen's face framed in the windshield of his car. He's not in a tank anymore. He's in a fast car. A Porsche or something, and she's frightened. She holds up her hands, and they're bound together.

"No!" I shout. "You can't have her!"

Dad smirks and says, "Then give me my son."

Richie grabs me in a death grip. I'll have to peel him off to give him to Dad. But before I can, Helen says, "No, Michael. It's okay. I'll be fine." Then she slams her foot on the gas, and the car hurtles off the edge of a cliff.

My scream tears the hospital apart. Nurses run in. They take the things Mrs. Mitchell gave me, which is when I really start screaming. Then they tie my hands and give me a shot.

When I wake later, it's daylight. Mrs. Mitchell's box is on the windowsill, and someone has freed my hands.

I push myself up, fight nausea, and eye the box. If it weren't sitting there, I'd have thought I dreamed Mrs. Mitchell's visit. But there it is. Proof that I'm not insane.

I slide my legs off my bed, ignore the throbbing, blinding pain in my head, and stagger over to the box. I lift the flaps slowly, as though I'm afraid something will jump out of it and attack me. What I'm really frightened of is disappointment. What if the picture of Helen is gone? Or worse, what if it doesn't look like how I remember her? Her eyes were green, right? I gave her some green earrings when we met in Moshie's store. I told her they'd bring out the green in her eyes, and they had. Right?

Or what if the copied pages are from her journal, and she says she hates me in it? That she was only leading me on to get even with her parents? What if I didn't know her at all?

I lug the box to my bed. It takes too much effort and makes dots appear before my eyes. When I'm settled and sure I won't pass out, I suck in a huge breath like I'm going to dive to the bottom of a lake, and look in the box.

In her senior picture, Helen's wearing the earrings I gave her. Her eyes sparkle green. Her hair glints like ripe wheat. Her skin glows with the remnants of her summer tan. Her laughing pose is pure Helen. I can almost hear Shelly joking. She could always make her laugh.

Here is the little drawing of her with Richie, chasing frogs last spring. "Thank you, Mrs. Mitchell," I say out loud. "It's a double gift." She probably didn't know it was Richie in the picture. Under that is a series of floral still lifes. Helen loved flowers, especially black-eyed Susans and lupines. She'd make bouquets from her mom's garden for me to draw or paint, and her arrangements were perfect.

I sort through dozens of snapshots, cards, and letters, and then I clutch the pile of copies. They're hard to read, probably because the originals were so light. The pages were decorated in pastels, and the words I'm struggling to read are handwritten. It begins, *Helen Ann Mitchell, born 2:33 p.m. on December 17. Weight: 7 pounds 3 ounces. Length: 20 inches.*

I fight to keep my tears from staining the pages. A nurse brings in a breakfast tray, sees what I'm doing, and leaves quietly. I don't eat. I read. I learn that her first word was *smile*, and she walked at ten and a half months. She hated green beans but loved sweet potatoes and squash. She had her shots on time, and her teeth came in *on schedule.*

But it isn't until I reach the next to the last page, after the descriptions of her birthday parties and her first day of kindergarten, that I come to the "Parents' Thoughts" and I discover why Mrs. Mitchell gave me this.

The photocopy reveals only a few lines. Helen, at four, was having trouble with hunting season and the dead deer strung up on tree branches, swing sets, porches. She asked her mom why God let the deer be killed. Mrs. Mitchell wrote, *I tried to explain about herd size and lack of predators to keep the deer under control, that they'd starve to death if they weren't hunted. Helen didn't believe me. She made this serious face and drifted off. I thought she fell asleep. Then, about fifteen minutes later, she announced that she knew why God let it happen. She said only the bad deer were shot as a punishment, like time-out, only worse. The good deer were allowed to live. It showed remarkable insight that she knew there was something wrong with hunting animals merely for the joy of killing. I wonder how her view will mature as she gets older.*

Written on this page in real ink is a note to me:

Maybe this is why she grabbed at life with both hands. I dismissed her theory then, because it's wrong. I told her goodness has nothing to do with hunting and which animal dies and which lives. Her death was the result of random violence. It had nothing to do with her personally or with us. She'd done nothing wrong. She loved life and questioned everything. She left more behind her in her short life than many do in decades of living.

Carry her in your heart. It's how we live on past death.
                                        Ruth Mitchell

I set down the papers and think of Mrs. Mitchell's story and her note. I knew how Helen's view had "matured," but I would probably never have the chance to tell Mrs. Mitchell.

I would try, though. I owed her that much.

35

Angela (Joshua)

". . . Amen."

Light dances like notes on a page before my drowned eyes. Words filter and break through ears plugged by water. My arms, last to fall still, don't even tense as I try to conduct the chorus. Always the music flows, like springwater coursing from the earth, pouring between rocks and over moss, rejoicing in the light.

Josh is here. I can't turn my head, but his shadow crosses my face, blocks the light at the window. His shadow is so thin, I can almost breathe it away.

I wish I could breathe my forgiveness to him.

It wasn't his fault, not really. I shouldn't have hidden the letter in the jewel case between the pages with the words for the I. Kyrie and the Gloria. I could have stopped playing the Mass. I knew he needed to study.

I made the choice to go into the water. I thought it wasn't deep enough, that I would reach the box before the letter was soaked through, it floated so nicely.

How was I to know it rested on the lips of the drainpipe? That the water was frigid, life-sucking? My legs grew numb, and I couldn't kick, couldn't walk. I lost my footing, then I went under. My hands found the pipe, and I worked up to its top, but I couldn't wrench the CD case from the pipe. The suction was too great. My head hurt with cold. I felt my hair wrapping around the pipe in the rising water, but I was so weak.

No, Josh shouldn't blame himself. The letter went undiscovered. Dad knocked the case off of the pipe with a huge rock. It sank, along with the letter, to the bottom of the pond. I hear Dad at night, throwing rocks, dirt, logs into the water, trying to make it give back what it took.

But it didn't take me. It took my body, yes, but not me. Now the weight of living is taking my body, and I can almost let go. If only I could see him one last time, but Mom has whispered of him, and he's in jail for something. Something to do with Helen.

It's been Helen I've seen the last two days. When I open my eyes, I see only colors, lights, shadows, forms, as though my brain can no longer piece things together.

But Helen it recognizes. She stands to the left of my bed, close to the ceiling. She's floating like an angel. For the longest time, I didn't know what she wanted. But I do now. She's waiting for me. Poor Helen. She doesn't seem to hear the music. I'll sing the Agnus Dei *to her.*

I open my lips, but my breath rattles.

Mom's head sinks to my bed, trapping my hair. I want to tug it free, but I can't move. I try again, and I sing. Helen moves closer and whispers Michael's name.

Mom sobs, and I rattle again. Gram's hand shadows my face. It waves down, then halfway up, then to my left, then to my right. Josh's shadow has fled.

I hit the glorious high-note vibrato, then drop into the last line. Helen's beside me. No, I'm beside Helen by the ceiling. We float, fluttering on the draft of air from the woodstove. I hear a chorus begin the Dona Nobis Pacem. *We move up the chimney with the smoke into the chill air. Dad and Josh are by the pond. Dad leans into him, buckles under the weight of my passing. The wind gusts as I join the chorus singing the* Ode to Joy.

Don't tell them, Josh. You don't know the truth anyway.

Go in peace.

36

MICHAEL

_____

"Contentment is wealth,
Forceful conduct is willfulness; . . ."

I'm living Ebenezer Scrooge's nightmare, I think, when I step out of the hospital bathroom to find Moshie standing by the window. He's my second ghostly visitor, and I can't imagine who would be the third.

I hesitate before speaking. I want to study Moshie, to see if Helen's death changed him. I also look for clues about his past and why he left.

Moshie clasps his hands behind him. He wears a familiar tie-dyed shirt that hangs loose around his hips. His pants are khakis, though, not the usual paint-splattered baggy jeans with holes everywhere. His beard, which Helen loved because it made him look like a dwarf of Middle Earth, has been trimmed to a respectable length. I touch my own hair, which was shorn to make me presentable. Whatever else Moshie's doing, he's trying to prove himself. But to whom?

My lips shake a tentative smile into the silence. I clear my throat and blurt, "I thought you'd left me." I don't want to be needy. It's time I walked on my own. I have leaned on too many people. Yet here I am, spouting off without even a hello.

He shuffles across the room, his head swaying with denial and grief. Then I'm in his arms, crushed against his chest. "I'm so sorry, Michael," he says. "For Helen, for your loss, for leaving you when you needed me. I didn't know where you were. I wouldn't have abandoned you if I had."

"You didn't abandon me." It's true. The only people who abandoned me are related by blood. Moshie's here, in the flesh. I was the one who ran away the day after Helen's death. "I left before anyone knew what happened. Dad kicked me out." I pause as he pushes me away so he can swab his eyes with a big handkerchief. He's the only person I know who uses those things.

"But I didn't come looking for you," he says. "I should have known something was wrong when you didn't bring in the commission for the Buffalo gallery. You would never have skipped out on something like that."

"I don't have the picture," I say. My head droops with guilt. I've let Moshie down.

"Little wonder," he says. He motions for me to get back in bed.

"I went to the apartment," Moshie says at last. "You were there, weren't you?"

"Yeah, I went there. I was looking for you."

"And you found my ghosts? You read the clippings?"

I nod, but say nothing. It's up to him to tell me or not.

"Helen knew, of course." Moshie straightens as though his back hurts. "Couldn't hide anything from her. Nosiest little sneak I ever loved."

"She knew? But then—"

"Why didn't she tell you?" He puts his hands on his knees and pushes himself straighter. "Because I asked her not to." He peers at me. "I didn't want you thinking I was a quitter, or a runaway. I didn't want to give you any reason to give up trying to improve yourself. I was afraid that if I told you the truth about who I was, you'd figure there was no point in working to escape your upbringing. But there is."

"There was," I correct. "I don't have a reason for living anymore. Even Richie's gone. It doesn't matter what I do."

"Oh? How is that?"

"Come on, Moshie, Helen's gone. She's dead. What is there to fight for?"

"And what about Michael Knight? Is he dead?"

I stare. "He doesn't matter. Never did."

"On the contrary. He's why I tried so hard to be a good sculptor, because I couldn't bear to see the disappointment in his eyes. Don't you understand? You have others who need you. You have yet to do what you were put on this earth for."

He's talking about my art. But I can't stand to hold a pencil. Since I left Pittsburgh, I haven't even tried to draw. "I'm not an artist," I mutter. "Never really was. I was a kid who tried to do something, but failed."

"That's nonsense. Art comes from pain, experience, and joy. It comes from living. You haven't begun to paint at the level you will eventually. You have a gift. Helen would never have wanted you to throw it away."

"She didn't have a problem with you throwing your talents away."

He nods. "I deserve that, but I didn't throw anything away. I changed. In a cowardly, desperate manner, but I changed for the better in the end. I should have faced my doubts. I shouldn't have run out on my wife and kid. I should have stood up and said, 'I can't take this anymore. I don't believe in it.' But I didn't." He rubs his face with both hands, then stares at his feet. "I'm trying to make up for that now."

I wait, but when he says nothing else, I have to ask, "What happened, Moshie?"

His face grays in the morning light. He shudders, spreads his hands, then says, "Yes, what happened? I was a judge on the Federal Court of Appeals. I handed down verdicts that said the world exists in black and white. I kept my face impassive, remained unimpressed by pleas from the shadowy figures that pressed close to my bench. I didn't look at them. To look meant I had to see, and that I couldn't do. Until." He pauses and lumbers to the window.

I can't see his face. His voice holds pain enough.

"She resembled Helen," he says. "She was young and, despite the scars on her face and arms, rather pretty in an unkempt sort of way. But—and for me this was a big but—she was a murderer. She'd killed the child God gave her. I'd put her in placement, you see, years earlier. Her mother felt that, when I'd taken her from them, she'd learned to hate. The idea that I'd failed this girl, and so many others, when I'd passed judgment on them, destroyed me. They came before me for ever-worsening crimes, but never for murder. Never for killing their own child in a fit of rage.

"I felt useless, a cog, guilty. Out of control, afraid God meant it to happen." He chokes and turns partway toward me. "I shouldn't talk like this."

"No," I say. "It's kind of how I feel about Helen's death. It's senseless, but, in a way, it's better than if they meant to kill her."

"Oh, this woman felt that punishing her child was all right," he says. "She thought it was the kid's fault for wetting the bed, for stumbling when she was hit and banging her head on the nightstand."

I cringe and think of Dad. What will happen to Richie when Dad punishes him?

But Moshie's not finished. "I sentenced her to life without parole. It was what the law said I had to do. But that night and every night afterward, her eyes haunted me, waking and sleeping. Could I have done something else so long ago when she'd been young? Could I have stopped the train then?"

I think of my mother. See her fall. What would have happened if she'd grabbed the ax from the woodpile and buried it in Dad's skull? Who would have been more guilty, him or her? And where would I be? There'd be no Richie. Maybe Helen would be alive. So many different possibilities from the actions of that single moment.

Silence drops over the room. I don't know what Moshie's thinking, if he's done. But I'm remembering how Mr. Mitchell had pulled Helen into the house the night he said we couldn't see each other anymore. His big, bigoted frame had blocked the sight of her as she screamed that she'd call me. That I shouldn't worry. She'd see me again if she had to run away to do it. Had he heard me yell to her? "No, don't do that. Stay there. Stay safe," I'd said. "He'll come around."

But he hadn't, and we'd resorted to sneaking, to taking advantage of occasions like Andy's party to be together.

Moshie sinks into the only chair. "I couldn't get past my doubts, my failure. One day, I stood up from my bench mid-trial, walked into my chambers, and out the door. I never went back. I left my car in one state, my clothes in another. I had money and talent. I let my hair grow. I sent divorce papers to my wife through a lawyer whom I swore to secrecy, and I settled here, sculpting and living in a gray zone. I financed my life at first with the interest from the savings accounts from my previous existence, then I did it with the sales of my art.

"You teenagers were an afterthought," he says. A smile almost touches his lips. "But you provided the perfect cover. You also made me think of things I'd never wanted to consider, like that people's lives drive them to the crimes they commit, that sometimes something is just a youthful indiscretion. I started helping kids make better choices, to avoid the dumb mistakes that could ruin their entire lives. I coached them on preserving their futures while living in the present.

"Then you arrived, and later Helen did." He chuckles.

What is he remembering that makes him laugh? I've had a hard time remembering the good times. They hurt worse than the bad ones.

"She was a born politician," he says. "She argued every point I made, saw through every convention to the hard truths. 'There's no reason for handguns, you know,' she said to me one day." His eyes become somber.

I can't help thinking, *No gun at the party; Helen lives.*

But Moshie isn't thinking of now. "Helen," he says, "had the passion of a prosecutor or an ideological senator. With her talent for argument and depth of feeling, I thought she could become president someday."

Instead she's dead, I think, bitterness rising. *It's such a waste.*

But Moshie continues, "When I found out about Helen's death, I went into my storage room. It's funny, the things you hang on to. I took out my robes, the framed degree I'd pulled off the wall in my chambers, and my gavel. I was thinking of how Helen made me feel, and I was wondering if I could go back. I was wondering if Saul Moshe Weinstein could make a difference in this world."

We sit in silence. It's almost as if he's making that decision again.

"I decided, Michael, that for Helen, I had to return. Even if it was just to draft motions in domestic-violence cases, I had to do something." He stares at me. "What will you do for Helen, Michael? What will you do to keep her memory alive and her life from being a waste?"

The question slams my mind into blankness. I shrug. Find Richie? Go to college? Become an art teacher like Mrs. Winthrop? One who really cares about kids and art? Or try to create paintings that show the world as it really is?

Moshie pats my knee. "I have a letter for you, with a proposition of sorts. Think about what I've said, what I've written, and let me know what you decide. Take your time. I'll wait." He stands.

Suddenly I don't want to be alone. I remember how Richie begged me to take him with me, and it's what I want to do now. Beg Moshie to take me with him. But I stay quiet. I reach for his letter and tuck it under my water pitcher.

"Never say good-bye," he always said. "It's like a curse. Say 'until we meet once more.' Then you know you'll see each other again."

True to his word, Moshie bends and hugs me, and without a word, walks out.

———————

The third ghost, from my present, arrives after lunch. "Michael?" says Mr. Lockwood.

I shake off my grogginess. "Hey!" I slide my aching body so I can sit up.

"Gave yourself a nasty concussion there." He peers at my head.

"Oh yeah?" No one said anything about a concussion, not even Moshie. I check the time. Four o'clock.

"They've monitored you closely. You'll be fine."

I nod, but waves of green wash over me.

He laughs. "That'll wear off. I had a bad concussion when I was cutting some timber once. Friend of mine saved my life, jerked me away so only a branch caught my head. Otherwise it would've been the trunk, and I wouldn't be here. So I know how you feel." He waits, studying the late-afternoon light.

"I'm sorry I didn't stay at the cabin," I say, because I can't keep quiet. "I had to get out."

"It's a good thing you left, as it turned out. They say you saved that boy's life. If you hadn't called 911, he might have died. The other kid was in shock and couldn't do more than confess. He'd lost a lot of blood."

He doesn't mention Victor.

"Listen, Michael? I've been doing some research. Well, actually, Mr. Harding has, and well, I don't think your dad killed your mom."

Everything flips. Color becomes black and white. Mr. Lockwood becomes a wraith with a gaping black mouth flapping open and shut, open and shut.

"That can't be right," I say.

"We traced your father's bank records and pay stubs. We located where you lived, found your birth certificate and your mother's name, then we traced her from the time she started using her married name until she stopped."

I don't like his pause. I will him to continue, but I also wish he'd go away. My mother's dead. That's why she never came for me.

"She opened a bank account in her married name after you moved here with your dad. It was in a town an hour from where you were born. She used that account for two years, and your father's pay was garnished and deposited into that account to support her."

"So he deposited money in an account in her name to make it look like she was alive."

"No, Michael." His voice is so gentle, almost loving.

"That has to be it."

"No." He waits for me to unclench my fists, to look at his steady blue eyes before he goes on. "There was other activity in the account, and we found other things she'd signed her name to—apartment leases, car insurance. She lived there for at least two years before she moved on."

"Where did she go?"

"That's hard to say. We checked Social Security, the IRS, everything, and there's no further record of her. She may have changed her name, married, moved overseas. She'd been living in Maine. It's not hard to imagine her immigrating to Canada. Or she may have died, although we found no proof of that. But, Michael, she did not die that night, the night you remember. You were enrolled in school for over a year before she vanished."

Vanished. Like a star lost in an unwatched sky. I think of the doe I saw once dead on the side of the road. She was curled up, head on her front legs. She'd looked so peaceful, as though asleep. Had she been hit by a car and hurt, so she'd curled up and died? Had she frozen to death? If so, why hadn't she run off to a warmer place than the cement road she'd died on? Or had she merely been resting in our world before disappearing back into hers? Because the next morning, when I drove past to work, she was gone.

Like that doe, I'll never know what happened to my mother. Mr. Lockwood watches me, his blue eyes so much like hers. Did I cry for her all those long years ago? I'm sure I did, and now I want to again. But should I cry for a woman who let her son go without a fight?

"Thanks for telling me." My voice breaks, and I hate myself for it. She doesn't deserve it. But maybe my tears aren't for her. I blink fast. Maybe they're for me, lost and alone. What would Helen have said when I told her this? She would have held me, told me that she loved me.

But Helen isn't here, either.

"I thought you deserved to know," Mr. Lockwood says. He takes my hand. "And, Michael, there's something else. A Mr.

Saul Moshe Weinstein has offered to pay your lawyer's fees. Do you know him?"

I'm stunned. He hadn't said anything about this during our visit. I glance at the table beside my bed. His letter lies, half-hidden by the water pitcher. "Yeah, I know Moshie."

"He called me two days ago. He said he knew you and wanted to help. He told me to tell you not to do anything until you read his letter. Promise me you won't?"

I gaze into his eyes. "Where would I go? What would I do?"

But he knows as well as I do. Or at least he knows who I'd go after. Richie. So he's never alone like this, so he knows his mother and grandparents and brother.

I have a brother and two friends. And I have to give something back to Mrs. Mitchell. I'm not entirely alone.

I shake Mr. Lockwood's hand. "I promise," I say.

He stands. "I'll be in touch." He looks out the window. His eyes are red-rimmed, tired. I've drained him these last few weeks. But beneath his sadness, I detect a hint of pride, in himself and in me. Was he giving back, too? Had someone helped him on his way to two pharmacies, a beautiful wife, and two daughters? "The cabin is yours for as long as you need."

I accept his kindness with a nod.

He leaves then without a word.

It takes me a while to pick up Moshie's letter. I slit the envelop with a trembling finger, then bend to read the shaking letter.

Dear Michael,

I know this has been a tough time, and I want to do every-thing in my power to help you, so after numerous inquiries,

I found the man who sheltered you in your time of strife.
I only wish I had done the same. He's a good man, this Mr.
Lockwood.

So, I'd like to offer you a home and a chance at college.
Don't think this is an entirely unselfish act. I miss you and
the teenagers who gathered in my shop. Mr. Lockwood has
said you're welcome to stay with him, but he says my request
should precede his, as we've known each other longer. Believe
me, I don't intend for you to give up your friendship with
Mr. Lockwood. I only intend to do what is best for you. If
you are interested in living with me, please contact me.

And, although I wish I could say anything else, my heart
bleeds at the loss of Helen, and I share at least some of your
grief. She will be missed more than you know.

Yours in friendship,
Saul Moshe Weinstein
Moshie

I lie in my hospital bed until dark creeps in, then the cloud-veiled moon and stars rise. I can't eat my dinner. The nurse scolds me like I'm a child.

But that's what I am. I'm a child who has finally realized that some adults can be trusted.

A retired judge would know how to find a lost boy like Richie, wouldn't he? And with Moshie, I could remember Helen. How we met on that absurdly defiant afternoon when she and Shelly barged into the world of tattoos, looking for drug paraphernalia and adventure. They never found the drug junk, but they found more adventure than either of them wanted. Poor Shelly. She's lost her best friend and her house. But she'll survive. She's so quick to adapt. It was her idea to come to the shop. I should thank her for introducing me to Helen, although she reeked of disapproval at the time.

But does Shelly regret introducing us? If Helen hadn't come into Moshie's shop that day, all smiles and kindness, without a trace of the snotty attitude I expected, we wouldn't have fallen in love. And she wouldn't have been with me that night.

Was her knowing love before she died worth it? Was I only an incidental part of her death? The part that decided where she died? What did that make Andy? A weapon in Fate's hand? Or the murderer I need him to be?

And if Fate's in charge, does that mean I'm not meant to have Richie with me? Would I have been a bad influence on him without Helen's death? Would I have drifted through life doing little, achieving nothing, being no one without her loss?

I can't believe that. Helen would have made me more than I can possibly be on my own.

What can I be with Moshie's help?

I stare at the phone, then pick it up. I won't be able to stay in the hospital forever. I need to decide what to do. I dial. When the gruff voice answers, I say, "Can you come and get me?"

His sobs are my answer.

37

JOSHUA

(Stand)

Mom comes into the room, her eyes circled with black like an ancient Egyptian's, except her circles aren't makeup. She brushes aside the curtain with her shoulder. She carries a tray with food and a little white cup.

"Time to eat." All the joy is gone from her voice. She sets the tray on the table under the window where Angela's sheet music used to be. "Come on, Josh. Eat."

She doesn't say, "Take your pill," but that's what she means. I stand by my bed and stare at the cup. Those little pills are supposed to take the voices away. To leave me with nothing. A voice sings in my mind, a voice I want to put to rest, but these pills won't do it. Only He can do that, and only in His time.

"Do you miss the voices?" Andy asked when I visited him at the detention center.

"Naw," I said. My hands ran up and down my arms, sliding

in and out of my shirtsleeves. I couldn't stop them. I couldn't tell Andy or anyone else about my hearing Angela's voice. Not him especially. Although Angela didn't write the name of the guy she loved in her journal, I know it was him.

But Andy needed to hear her name, so I said, "The voices used to make me feel closer to Angela."

He nodded and waited, his hands clasped on the table. He wasn't wearing an orange jumpsuit like I'd expected. His clothes were a soft blue, like washed denim.

"She's dying, you know." I tried to meet his eye but couldn't. If he cared for her, a part of him would be dying, too. But maybe he no longer felt what he had when she'd played the piano for him. She had been gone from him for a long time.

But he sank lower in his chair, and his head bobbed forward. "I miss her," he said. Two drops fell onto the table beneath Andy's swaying head, then a third, and a fourth.

And I forgave him for not telling me that he loved my sister. I tried to stifle a sob, which only made it louder in the small room. I didn't mention Angela again. I didn't say anything else, as a matter of fact, until the guard said it was time to leave. I asked him for a few more minutes.

He frowned, then gave me a curt nod.

I leaned forward. "Hey, buddy, I'll visit as often as I can. At least once a week. And I'll be waiting for your release. I'll help you then."

By helping him, maybe I'll help myself. I had my Bible, and I drew it out. He watched me with an almost hungry look, but he couldn't meet my eyes. One hundred and fifty Psalms. One per visit, then maybe the Gospels. I began with the twenty-third.

When I finished, a feeling of rightness swept over me, as though I'd been told that this is what I needed to do. Andy traced the gilt lettering and design on the Bible's red cover. Then he drew his hand away. Maybe next time he'll open it and look for his own comfort. Maybe someday he'll ask for his own copy.

"You'll make a good priest," he said softly. He stood when the guard coughed. "You know that, Josh?"

I nodded and muttered, "Thanks." Then I let my best friend, the murderer, leave without knowing his best friend is a liar and murderer, too.

But Andy's not a murderer. The court accepted his self-defense plea in Victor's death and gave him the lightest manslaughter charge for Helen's. He'll be thirty at the most—probably younger—when he gets out. Maybe he'll still go to college. If I make it through seminary, we'll graduate together.

———

I go to the table so Mom doesn't have to ask me to eat again. I pick up the little cup in one hand and the glass of juice in the other. On her side of the room, Angela rattles. Her arms don't move, not even in that slow swimming motion she did throughout the Bad Time. She hasn't touched her tube once since I came home from the hospital, my ribs cracked, my eyes black, my nose broken, and my head a mess of bruises and one huge gash.

Behind me someone mutters the rosary. Father Paul comes by twice daily, but this is Gram. She sits beside Angela and prays endlessly. She expects me to join her, but I can't. It's hard enough listening to Angela die; I don't think I can watch her. When it's over, I can move on. I'll tell Mom about what happened between Angela and me; I hope she can forgive me. I have to tell Dad, too, but I'll do that second, so if he kills me, Mom'll know the truth. It's been hard on her having no reason for why Angela went into the pond.

I swallow the pill and gaze out the window. Last night, I went up to my church. I dragged every rock from my altar to the pond and threw them in one by one. The *splooshes* split the quiet. If my parents heard, they didn't come out or say anything. Funny, but the pond doesn't look any shallower.

I chew my sandwich as the rattle grows louder. Mom cries beside Angela, her forehead resting on Angela's golden hair.

The pond ripples in a ruffling wind. Dad sits on the bank, a shovel sunk into the gouged earth beside him, his head in his hands. Below him gapes a gash wide enough for a truck to drive down, but the pond looks as deep as ever.

It won't change anything, Dad. The spring keeps flowing, filling, covering the ground. Your digging won't change that any more than my pledge did.

I go outside and sit next to him. I listen to him sob his anger into the mud. I imagine telling him about that day with Angela. His face will shut against me, and I'll taste the blood of fear and rage when he punches me.

But maybe he won't do that. Maybe he'll only cry, like he's doing now.

We sit and watch our tiny house, whose wood-burning stove sends curls of smoke into the cold November wind. The smoke billows and scatters. In my mind, Angela's singing crests and falls, flowing like the clouds.

Then there's silence.

I start for the house, but stop before I get there, certain it's over. I look up and see shapes in the smoke. Dancing figures. The wind carries them toward me, and as they swoop low, Bach's *Ode to Joy* crashes into my mind.

Warmth and joy flow through me, and I grab Dad's arm, try to get him to see. He only stares at me, then clutches me in his grief. Wispy fingers drape his head, and his sobs ease, but they don't cease. I want to touch the outstretched hand, but Dad has pinned my arms to my sides. I lift my face.

"Don't tell them, Josh," Angela says. *"You don't know the truth anyway. Go in peace."*

I shake my head, remembering the pill and what the psychiatrist told me: "It's all in my head. It's wish fulfillment—a sign of a troubled mind."

In the instant it takes to glance at Dad and back, Angela's gone. Tears swirl my vision.

"Good-bye, Angela," I say.

Dad's grip loosens, then he plunges his face into his muddy hands.

I blink fast and walk to the water's edge. The wind races across the shimmering surface piling waves before it. The waves break on the lip of a rock. My altar, washed clean of Victor's curses, rises above the water.

"Come inside, Josh," Dad says. "Your mother needs us."

I face him.

His arm is outstretched. His fingers tremble.

"There's a rock out there," I say. "Can you see it?"

Dad's tired eyes register surprise, then resignation. He glances at the mud caking his boots, pants, and shirt. "Little wonder."

"But it wasn't there a moment ago," I insist.

Dad's head swivels from me to the pond and back. His eyes look hungry and lost. "No," he says. "It wasn't."

I wade into the pond. It *is* shallower. The water doesn't rise above my knees. I want to shout, *We've made a difference!*

Then I'm at the rock. I touch it, and my fingers leave dark splotches on its dry surface. Music flows back into my mind, finding the hurts, the guilt, and easing them.

I hear splashing behind me. I turn and see Dad slogging toward me, panic convulsing his face. "Josh!" he screams.

Why does the water seem deeper on him? I step off the rock and walk back to him. He hugs me, claws at me, chest heaving. "Don't ever do that again!" he shouts. "Don't ever come near this pond again." He half carries me out of the water and sets me on the ground.

He touches my dry clothes, my face, my eyes. "Josh?" he asks.

But I see only the rock, hear only another question. "I won't falter," I answer.

This time, my pledge is real.

38

MICHAEL

"Not losing one's rightful place is to endure,
To die but not be forgotten is longevity."

Moshie's meeting me in town in a few hours. Below me, the forest, some logging paths, and a few houses sprawl. Above me, the clouds look like a child's pale blond hair blowing across its smooth cheek. I'm almost ready to go, almost eager to leave.

But the urge to flee from Moshie's help, to run after Richie, is huge. Some of it is fear of the future and of failure. What if I flunk out of school? What if Moshie and I can't get along? Can I accept that someone thinks I'm worth fighting for? It's been a long time since anyone besides Helen thought that.

And what about Richie? I'll never stop looking for him. Mr. Lockwood gave me a topographical map of Montana. I pegged it up over his fireplace and studied it for hours. So few roads, so many winding rivers and lonely valleys. And what if they didn't go there? What if Dad told Richie Montana, but went to Texas? Mr. Lockwood hired a private detective to find him, but Dad had left no impression on the landscapes through which he passed.

What if he went to Canada? Or Mexico?

"Richie? What should I do? Helen? Where do I go? To Moshie and a future that will take me out of all this? Or do I hunt my past to save Richie's future?"

But what would I do if I found him? Dad wouldn't let me take Richie without a fight. He'd call the cops. I don't have custody of Richie, so I'd be accused of kidnapping. Maybe I should give Richie's note to Kathy, Richie's mom, and let her follow his trail?

If I go with Moshie today, does that mean I have to give up on finding Richie? No. Just as he'd never ask me to forget Helen, Moshie would never make me give up on Richie. I'll never find him by myself. I can try with Moshie, though.

"Every summer and vacation I'll search," I shout at the dull brown hill opposite my perch. A hawk squawks and flies off a dead tree. "Every job I take will be a way to find you, Richie. I'll never quit. I'll write letters to town halls and schools, asking if they've seen you. I'll plaster Montana with posters, and then I'll do the same with other states. I'll get your face on every milk carton in the country until I find you. Don't give up, Richie. I'll find you. I promise."

And when I do, what do I do about my father?

Rage fires my gut, but it quickly splutters out. I see Victor's sullen body lying in the dirt, hear Andy's confession, listen again to Moshie telling us not to act rashly, to think before we do anything.

I don't know what the answer is, but it's not violence. That's what took Helen, killed Victor, drove Josh insane, and landed Andy in jail. It may have been what kept my mother from me. Was she afraid I'd turn out like Dad?

Beating myself up isn't the answer, either, but I can't help it. I have nothing else to do for the three hours until I'm supposed to meet Moshie.

From my pack I take the bundle of sketches Mrs. Mitchell returned to me and flip through them. When I come to a sketch of a single violet cupped in Helen's palm, I stop. That's what her hand looked like! Her long, slender fingers, her trim, squared-off nails, the scar from a fight with her sister, Susie. It drowns me in vivid detail. All those nights I struggled to capture the turn of her fingers, the curve of her wrist, and here it is.

I glance at my watch. I have time.

I have the paints out and the design blocked before I'm aware of it. The hand first, then the violet. Springwater runs from a hole at the bottom of the hill. I scramble down and drink before filling a container for my paints. The water's cool and earthy, clean in a way that the water at Mr. Lockwood's pharmacy isn't. Moshie's water in Buffalo won't taste like this, either.

I drink again, stare at the hand resting on the paper. I see the soft mellow leaves fluttering around it, hear Helen's laugh. She'd dragged me through the woods for hours that afternoon. We'd only been seeing each other for a month, and by that I mean we'd been meeting at Moshie's. He'd beam at us, then slip behind the beaded curtain that separated his back room from the storefront. We'd perch on stools behind the counter, wait on customers, help them select tattoos and T-shirts, and talk.

The hike had been our first "date." It was the time of peepers, daffodils, and violets, when fawns spring unexpectedly into glades, bawl at intruders, then dart back to the does in the shad-ows. It was the time of mud and fast-flowing water tumbling from creases in the hillsides, scattering colored prisms through sunlight, then plummeting into a stream. Leeks perfumed the air with their pungent scent. Last year's brambles had been flattened by the snow.

Helen had never seen a fiddle fern, swirled like a spiraled lollipop. She'd never seen the little yellow flowers Dad hadn't identified for me. Maybe he didn't notice flowers. Maybe they were waste products to him. But to me, they were beautiful. Helen found their name in her flower guide. They were called trout lilies, and she loved them second only to the white, purple, or lavender violets that dotted hills and path both.

"Oh, Michael! I can't believe I've lived here all my life and never tramped in the woods like this." She touched a huge lichen on the decayed body of a tree that had died twenty-odd years ago. It'd probably sprouted two hundred years before that. Out of the pulpy, insect-ridden trunk grew a small maple, probably five years old. The deer had eaten it during the winter, so it was short and fat at the base, but it had a half-dozen sticks poking every which way from its sides. "It looks funny," Helen said.

"But it's going to make it," I said. "It's made it past the worst of the grazing—it has a few twigs left from last year. If we came back every month this spring, it'd be unrecognizable, it will grow so fast. Next it will have to stand up to bucks rubbing antlers against it, or trees falling on it. Ice storms are a risk, too. At a certain size, trees seem indestructible, but see that big cherry? It fell last winter. Moles gnawed on its bark under the snow until, in spring, the sap couldn't find a path to its branches. Girdled, it blew over in a storm."

"Oh, that's too bad." Helen looked sad.

I took her hand. "That's life," I said.

She nodded, then bent over a perfect violet huddling at the foot of the little maple. She reached as though to pluck it, hesitated, then cupped the flower in her hand and bent to examine it. When she turned, her face glowed. I wasn't feeling too confident about drawing faces then, not having mastered lips, but hands, as difficult as they are, were my favorite. I pulled out my sketch pad and made a quick rendering of the tender curve of her hand cherishing the flower.

When she saw my pad, she froze.

And I quit sketching.

"Don't stop," she said. "I'll hold my position."

"I'm done," I lied. I didn't want to tell her that her hand looked forced, unnatural now.

She bounded over to see at what I'd drawn. "But it's a rough sketch," she said. "It's not done."

"Nothing's ever done. But I'm satisfied. Do you want it?" I asked. I hadn't given her a picture yet, and she whooped in delight.

She didn't rip it out, though. "You carry it. I have no place to keep it."

Like that afternoon, the feeling that I am totally, irrevocably present in this moment of paint and color, form and structure, takes me. I'm free. I'm in the sky, judging and adjusting shadows, hearing Helen, feeling her touch, knowing nothing's more important than this moment, this completion, this creation of a perfect picture. But I'm also aware of the earth, the pain, the darkness, the future, and the past, the shadows that make the light bearable. Everything melds and blends, wavers and sings. The world has drawn its breath.

When I focus on the living greens and gentle violets, the flushing pinks and vibrant peaches of the painting in my hands, the universe exhales. I recognize the painting, yet I don't. My hands did this, yet I stare at it in wonder because I could not tell how it was done. A part of me wants to throw it to the wind, to give it back to the Power that lent me the ability to step out of the world, if only for a time, and find Helen again. Find peace. Find solace.

But I won't sacrifice my painting to the elements. Other ways exist to pay a debt, and other debts await payment.

————————

Mr. Lockwood's four-wheeler stands by the cabin. I'll leave it at his friend's, Mr. Trumble's. I stroke the watercolor of Helen's hand cupped around a solitary violet. It has dried quickly in the wind. Disbelief that I did it crashes over me, but before I can change my mind, I roll it up with a short letter. The letter tells about Helen's wish that the coyotes could be reintroduced to keep the deer herd in check so there would be no need to hunt. I address the tube to Ruth Mitchell. I hope she'll understand why I wrote it. I heft my duffel bag, grab the tube, and lock the cabin.

The four-wheeler's tires skitter over the newly frozen earth as I roar down the river path to town and Moshie. My future stretches, empty and formless, before me. But behind me lies the rock of my life. Helen. I will lean on her forever. I'll never truly leave.

Blessing/Recessional

Yea, though I walk through the valley of the shadow
  of death,
I will fear no evil:
for You are with me . . .
Surely goodness and mercy shall follow me
all the days of my life:
and I will dwell in the house of the Lord for ever.
PSALM 23: 4–6

It must be past 2:00 a.m., and my head aches. Too many wine coolers. I edge my elbow under me so I can see if Michael's sleeping. He is. His chest rises and falls in the deep sleep half caused by the alcohol and half by what we've done. His face is turned toward me, his mouth slightly open. I wipe the tiny drop of spit resting on the edge of his lips, and he stirs. I pull my hand away and smile as he closes and opens his mouth, then turns onto his side and reaches for me.

I lie back, feeling the weight of his arm across my belly and wishing Mom and Dad could know him like I do. His wit, his gentleness.

I'm smiling again, feeling like an idiot for wishing my parents could see me now. They'd kill me, but they don't understand anything. No pain comes from our wish to join our lives. I could still go to college first. Michael will wait through centuries for me if he has to. He's told me so.

The noise downstairs is muted, mostly male. There's a guffaw and a *thump, thump, thump* of footsteps going down the stairs. I roll under Michael's arm, glad that he's with me and not the rest of the party.

But what's left of the party is breaking up. Shelly's distinctive horse laugh whinnies on the porch. Her newest flame, Tom, tells her she'll wake the deer if she doesn't quiet down. She only laughs again, louder, and he says, "Christ," in a muted shout. She's skipping away from him, I'm sure. She's such a nutcase. She's probably standing on the far side of the car, threatening to bolt into the black woods. But she won't. She'll taunt him into chasing and catching her, then she'll melt into him, and he'll shove her into the car, beer bottle and all.

The car door slams. I stretch my legs. How many kids are left? Grabbit is here for sure, since it's his dad's cabin. That means that Munger probably is, too. And Josh Stedman.

Flexing my cramped leg makes me realize what woke me. I have to pee. Not bad, but enough so that it's uncomfortable to lie with Michael's arm draped on my belly. I roll so that his arm falls across my hip, but that seems to cause a letdown somewhere in the kidney track. I have to go bad.

Downstairs things are quieter since the departure of Tom and Shelly. There's a muffled conversation, but even the music is low. Maybe they're bedding down for the night. I don't want anyone to see me half-dressed, so that means I have to find some clothes—my clothes. I don't want to hear Andy's snickers if I

appeared in Michael's flannel shirt and oil-stained pants. Where
is the bathroom anyway?

Sitting up has eased the pressure on my bladder somewhat, so
I debate staying warm and cozy with Michael, but then I remember what that woman at the clinic told me when I went for the
antibiotics last time.

"You can do a few things to help avoid developing urinary-
tract infections. Drink cranberry juice. Its acidity seems to help
preserve the health of the urinary system." Whatever that
includes. "Be sure to wipe from front to back. And urinate as
soon after intercourse as you can. That's been proven to help."

She knew about the intercourse stuff because she's the same
nurse who gave me my Pills. I blushed, I know I did, because she
patted my knee just like the first time I told her I needed birth
control and my face heated the room to about a hundred degrees.

So I have to pee, but I've slept for how long? I glance at the
clock. At least an hour. Will it do any good if I go now instead
of waiting fifteen minutes to be sure the other guys are asleep?

My foot finds the softness of my sweater on the floor, and my
jeans are right beneath it. Years of good training keeps me from
throwing my clothes around, even in the throes of passion.
Heck, my jeans are folded. I might as well go. If I stay here toss-
ing and turning, I'll probably wake Michael, and he has to go to
work early tomorrow.

I pull on my sweater and jeans, not bothering with bra and
underpants. I press my lips to Michael's forehead and say, "I love
you." The night receives my blessing, but Michael doesn't stir. I
hope he won't be too hungover to work tomorrow. He'll get

fired if he doesn't watch it. I touch his hair, which curls against his cheek in a wild cascade of black froth. "I'll be right back," I whisper.

I bump into the dresser as I slide-step my way across the unfamiliar floor to the door. I glance at Michael, but he's sleeping. I smile, then open the door.